Cyclamen:
Diffidence

As an undercover espionage agent, Lady Hannah Rothchild could change her image as quickly as a chameleon changed the color of its skin, and her personality in Cordina was one of retiring diffidence, cool and shy. Her mission to protect the royal family was carefully plotted, but the plans didn't include the hot-blooded assault of the prince of playboys—the playboy prince!

NORA ROBERTS
LANGUAGE OF LOVE

Love has a language all its own, and for
centuries, flowers have symbolized
love's finest expression.
Discover the language of flowers
—and love—
in this romantic collection of 48 favorite
books by bestselling author Nora Roberts.

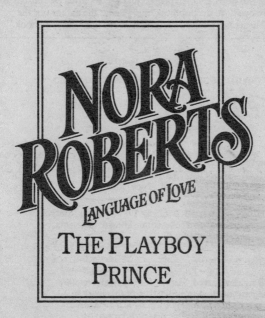

NORA ROBERTS

LANGUAGE OF LOVE

THE PLAYBOY PRINCE

Silhouette® Books

Published by Silhouette Books New York

America's Publisher of Contemporary Romance

For Tara Bell,
with hope that her wishes come true

? TEL

SILHOUETTE BOOKS
300 East 42nd St., New York, N.Y. 10017

RECYCLED PAPER · RECYCLED PAPER

THE PLAYBOY PRINCE © 1987 by Nora Roberts.
First published as a Silhouette Intimate Moments.

Language of Love edition published February 1994.

ISBN: 0-373-51039-X

Printed in U.S.A.

Chapter One

The stallion plunged over the crest of the hill, digging hard into the earth and kicking up smoke. At the peak, he reared, powerful forelegs pawing the air. For an instant, horse and rider were silhouetted against the bright afternoon sky. One looked as dangerous as the other.

Even as hooves touched earth, the rider's knees pressed to the stallion's side and sent them both recklessly racing down the sheer incline. The track there was smooth, but hardly gentle with a wall of rock on one side and a drop into space on the other. They took it at full speed and gloried in it.

Only a madman rode with such arrogant disregard for life and limb. Only a madman, or a dreamer.

"*Avant*, Dracula." The command was low and challenging as was the laughter that followed. The tone was one of a man who considered fear a banquet and speed the wine.

Birds, startled by the thunderous pounding of hooves on dirt, flew from the trees and bushes on the cliff above to wheel screaming into the sky. Their noise was soon lost in the distance. When the path veered to the left, the stallion took it without a pause. The edge of the road gave way to cliffs that spilled sharply for seventy feet to the white rocks and blue sea. Pebbles danced off the dirt to shower soundlessly into the empty spaces.

The rider glanced down but didn't slow. He never even considered it.

From that height, there was no scent of the sea. Even the sound of waves crashing was indistinct, like thunder far off and still harmless. But from that height, the sea held a danger and mystique all of its own. Every year she claimed her tribute in the lives of men. The rider understood this, accepted this, for so it had been since the beginning of time. So it would continue to be. At times like this he put himself in the hands of fate and backed his bet with his own skill.

The stallion needed no whip, no spur to drive him faster. As always, his master's excitement and confidence were enough. They tore down the twisting path until the sea roared in their ears and the cry of gulls could at last be heard.

To the onlooker, it might seem the horseman was fleeing from devils or racing to a lover. But anyone seeing his face would know it was neither.

If there was a gleam in the dark eyes, it wasn't one of fear or anticipation. It was challenge. For the moment, and the moment only. Speed whipped the man's dark hair as freely as the horse's dark mane.

The stallion was fifteen hands of coal-black energy, wide at the chest, powerful at the neck. The horse's hide glistened with sweat, but his breathing was strong and even. Astride him, the rider sat erect, his tanned, narrow face glowing. His mouth, full and sculpted, was curved in a smile that spoke of both recklessness and pleasure.

As the path leveled, the stallion's stride lengthened. Here, they passed whitewashed cottages where clothes flopped on lines in the sea breeze. Flowers crowded for space in tidy lawns and windows were opened and unscreened. The sun, still high in the sky after noon, flashed its brilliant light. Without slackening, without needing his master's light hands on the reins to guide him, the stallion sprinted for a hedge as high as a man's waist.

Together, they soared over it.

In the distance were the stables. As there were danger and deadly attraction in the cliffs behind, so were there peace and order to the scene ahead. Red and white, and tidy as the lawns surrounding them, the buildings added another touch of charm to a landscape of cliffs and greenery. Fences criss-crossed to form paddocks where horses were being exercised with far less drama than Dracula.

One of the grooms stopped circling a young mare on a lead when he heard the stallion's approach. Crazy as a loon, he thought—but not without grudging respect. This horse and this rider, merged together in a blare of speed, were a common sight. Even so, two grooms waited at attention for the stallion to slow to a halt.

"Your Highness."

His Highness, Prince Bennett of Cordina slid off Dracula's back with a laugh that echoed the recklessness. "I'll cool him down, Pipit."

The old groom with the slight limp stepped forward. His weathered face was passive, but he passed his gaze over both prince and stallion, checking for any sign of harm. "Your pardon, sir, but a message came down from the palace while you were out. Prince Armand wishes to see you."

Not without regret, Bennett handed the reins to the waiting groom. Part of the pleasure of the ride was the hour he normally spent walking and brushing down the stallion. If his father had sent for him, he had no choice but to forgo pleasure for duty.

"Walk him thoroughly, Pipit. We've had a long run."

"Yes, sir," said the groom who'd spent three-quarters of his life with horses. Among his duties had been seating Bennett on his first pony. At sixty, with one leg game from a fall, Pipit remembered the energy of youth. And the passion. He patted Dracula's neck and found it damp. "I'll see to it myself, Your Highness."

"Do that, Pipit." But Bennett loitered long enough to loosen the cinches. "Thanks."

"No thanks necessary, sir." With a quiet grunt, Pipit hefted the saddle from the stallion's back. "Isn't another man here who has the nerve to deal with the devil." He murmured in French as the horse began to dance in place. In moments, Dracula settled again.

"And there isn't another man I'd trust with my best. An extra scoop of grain wouldn't hurt him this evening."

Pipit took the compliment as no less than his due. "As you say, sir."

Still restless, Bennett turned to walk from the stables. He could have used the extra hour to cool himself down as well. Riding fast, riding reckless, satisfied only part of his thirst. He needed the movement, the speed, but most of all, he needed the freedom.

For nearly three months he'd been tied firmly to the palace and protocol, the pomp and procedure. As second in line to Cordina's throne, his duties were sometimes less public than his brother, Alexander's, but rarely less arduous. Duties, obligations, had been a part of his life since birth, and were normally taken as a matter of course. Bennett couldn't explain to himself, much less anyone else, why some time during the last year he'd begun to fret and chafe against them.

Gabriella saw it. Bennett thought perhaps his sister even understood it. She, too, had always had a thirst for freedom and privacy. She'd gained a portion of that two years before when Alexander had married Eve, and the weight of responsibility had shifted.

Still she never shirked, Bennett thought as he passed through the palace's garden doors. If she was needed, she was there. She still gave six months of every year to the Aid for Handicapped Children while keeping her marriage vital and raising her children.

Bennett dug his hands into his pockets as he climbed the stairs that would take him to his father's office. What was wrong with him? What had happened in the last few months that made him want to slip quietly out of the palace some night and run? Anywhere.

He couldn't shake off the mood, but he managed to tame it as he knocked on his father's door.

"Entrez."

The prince wasn't behind his desk as Bennett had expected, but was seated beside a tea tray at the window. Across from him was a woman who rose to her feet at Bennett's entrance.

As a man who appreciated women of any age, of any form, he took an easy survey before turning to his father. "I'm sorry to interrupt. I was told you wished to see me."

"Yes." Armand merely sipped his tea. "Some time ago. Prince Bennett, I would like to introduce Lady Hannah Rothchild."

"Your Highness." Her gaze swept down as she curtsied.

"A pleasure, Lady Hannah." Bennett took her hand, summing her up in seconds. Attractive in a quiet way. He preferred less subtlety in women. British from her accent. He had an affection for the French. Slim and neat. Invariably, the more voluptuous caught his eye. "Welcome to Cordina."

"Thank you, Your Highness." Her voice was indeed British, cultured and quiet. He met her gaze briefly so that he saw her eyes were a deep and glowing shade of green. "Yours is a beautiful country."

"Please, sit, my dear." Armand gestured her back to her chair before he lifted another cup to pour. "Bennett."

Hannah, with her hands folded in her lap, noticed Bennett's quick look of dislike at the teapot. But he sat and accepted the cup.

"Lady Hannah's mother was a distant cousin of yours," Armand began. "Eve became acquainted with her when she and your brother visited England recently. At Eve's invitation, Lady Hannah has agreed to stay with us as Eve's companion."

Bennett could only hope he wouldn't be expected to escort the lady. She was pretty enough, though she dressed like a nun in a gray, high-collared dress that came a discreet two inches below her knees. The color did nothing for her pale, British complexion. Her eyes saved her face from being plain, but with her dark blond hair pulled back so severely from her face, she put him in mind of the old Victorian companions or governesses. Dull. But he remembered his manners and treated her to an easy, companionable smile.

"I hope you enjoy your stay as much as we'll enjoy having you."

Hannah gave him a solemn look in return. She wondered if he was aware, and thought he was, of how dashing he looked in casual riding clothes. "I'm sure I'll enjoy it immensely, sir. I'm flattered the Princess Eve invited me to stay with her while she awaits the birth of her second child. I hope to give her the companionship and help she needs."

Though his mind was on other matters, Armand offered a plate of frosted cookies. "Lady Hannah has been very generous to give us her time. She's quite a scholar and is currently working on a series of essays."

Figures, Bennett thought, and sipped at the hated tea. "Fascinating."

The smallest of smiles touched Hannah's lips. "Do you read Yeats, sir?"

Bennett shifted in his chair and wished himself back to his stables. "Not extensively."

"My books should be here by the end of the week. Please feel free to borrow anything you like." She rose again, keeping her hands folded. "If you would excuse me, Your Highness, I'd like to see to the rest of my unpacking."

"Of course." Armand rose to lead her to the door. "We'll see you at dinner. Be sure to ring if you require anything."

"Thank you, sir." She curtsied, then turned to extend the courtesy to Bennett. "Good afternoon, Your Highness."

"*Bonjour*, Lady Hannah." Bennett waited for the door to close behind her before dropping onto the arm of his chair. "Well, she should bore Eve to tears within a week." Ignoring the tea, he took a handful of the small iced cookies. "What could Eve have been thinking of?"

"Eve became very fond of Hannah during her two weeks in England." Armand walked to a scrolled cabinet and, to Bennett's relief, took out a decanter. "Hannah is a well-bred young woman of excellent family. Her father is a highly respected member of the British Parliament." The brandy was deep and rich. Armand poured it sparingly.

"That's all well and good, but—" Bennett stopped abruptly as he reached for the snifter. "Oh good God, Father, you're not thinking of trying for a match here? She's hardly my type."

Armand's firm mouth softened with a smile. "I think I know that well enough. I can assure you Lady Hannah was not brought here to tempt you."

"She could hardly do that in any case." Bennett swirled the brandy, then sipped. "Yeats?"

"There are some who believe literature extends beyond equestrian handbooks." Armand drew out a cigarette. There was a knot of tension at the base of his neck. He forced it to concentrate there rather than allowing it to spread.

"I prefer the useful rather than poetry about unrequited love or the beauty of a raindrop." When that made him feel small and ungracious, Bennett relented. "But in any case, I'll do whatever I can to make Eve's new friend welcome."

"I never doubted it."

His conscience soothed, Bennett moved on to more important matters. "The Arabian mare should foal by Christmas. I'm betting it's a colt. Dracula will breed strong sons. I have three horses that should be ready to show in the spring, and another I think should be taken to the Olympic trials. I'd like to arrange that within the next few weeks so that the riders will have more time to work with the horse."

Armand gave an absent nod and continued to swirl his brandy. Bennett felt the familiar push of impatience rising and fought it down. He was well aware that the stables weren't high on his father's list of priorities. How could they be with internal affairs, foreign affairs, and the very tricky politics within the Council of the Crown?

Yet, didn't there have to be something more? The horses not only gave pleasure, but added a certain prestige when the Royal House of Cordina possessed one of the finest stables in Europe. For himself, it was what he considered his only true contribution to his family and country.

He'd worked for the stables as hard and as menially as any groom or stable boy. Over the years, he'd studied everything he could about breeding. To his delight, he'd found within himself a natural skill that had added spark to his education. Within a short time, Bennett had turned a good stable into one of the best. In another decade, he was confident it would have no equal.

There were times when Bennett needed to discuss his horses and his ambitions with someone other than a stable hand or another breeder. Still, he understood, and always had, that that person would rarely be his father.

"I take it this isn't the time to discuss it." Bennett took another small sip of brandy and waited for his father to reveal whatever weighed on his mind.

"I'm sorry, Bennett, I'm afraid it isn't." The father felt regret. The prince could not. "Your schedule this next week. Can you tell me about it?"

"Not really." The restlessness was back. Rising, Bennett began to pace from one window to another. How close the sea seemed and yet how far away. He wished for a moment that he was on a ship again, a hundred miles from any land, with a storm brewing on the horizon. "I know that I have to go into Le Havre at the end of the week. The *Indépendance* is coming in. There's a meeting with the Farmers' Cooperative and a couple of luncheons. Cassell fills me in each morning. If it's important I can have him type up the highlights for you. I'm sure I'm cutting at least one ribbon."

"Feeling closed in, Bennett?"

With a shrug, Bennett tossed off the last of his brandy. Then the easy smile returned. Life, after all, was too short to complain about. "It's the ribbons that do it. The rest, at least, seems worthwhile."

"Our people look to us for more than governing."

Bennett turned from the window. Behind him the sun was high and bright. Whatever he might sometimes wish in his secret heart, the royalty he'd been born with cloaked him. "I know, Papa. The problem is I don't have Alexander's patience, Brie's serenity or your control."

"You might need them all soon." Armand set his glass down and faced his son. "Deboque will be released from prison in two days."

Deboque. Even the name caused fury to churn in Bennett's stomach. François Deboque. The man by whose orders his sister had been kidnapped. The man who had planned assassination attempts on both his father and his brother.

Deboque.

Bennett pressed a finger to the scar just below his left shoulder. He'd taken a bullet there, and the trigger had been pulled by Deboque's lover. For Deboque. By Deboque.

The bomb planted just over two years before in the Paris Embassy had been meant for his father. Instead it had killed Seward, a loyal assistant, leaving a woman widowed and three children fatherless. That, too, had been Deboque's doing.

And in all the years, nearly ten now since Gabriella's kidnapping, no one had proved Deboque's involvement in the kidnapping, the conspiracies or the murders. The best investigators in Europe, including Bennett's brother-in-law, had been brought in, but none of them had proved that Deboque had pulled the strings.

Now, within days, he would be free.

There was no doubt in Bennett's mind that Deboque would continue to seek revenge. The Royal Family was his enemy if for no other reason than he'd been held in a Cordinian prison for over a decade. Neither was there any doubt that during that decade, he'd continued to deal in drugs, weapons and women.

No doubt, and no proof.

Guards would be added. Security would be tightened. Interpol would continue its work, as would the International Security System. But both Interpol and the ISS had been trying to nail Deboque with murder and conspiracy to murder for years. Until he was gotten under control and the strings to his organization severed, Cordina and the rest of Europe were vulnerable.

Hands in pockets, Bennett strode out to the garden. At least they'd dined *en famille* that evening. It had relieved some strain, even though little could be said in front of Eve's new friend. He doubted if anyone that quiet and prim would have picked up on any tension around the table. She had answered when spoken to and nursed one glass of wine throughout the meal.

He would have wished her back to England a dozen times if he hadn't seen how good she actually was for Eve. His sister-in-law was three months pregnant with her second child and didn't need the additional strain of talk of Deboque. Two years before she'd nearly been killed protecting Alexander. If Lady Hannah could keep Eve's mind off Deboque, even for a few hours a day, it would be worth the inconvenience of having her in the palace.

He needed to talk with Reeve. Bennett drove his balled fists into his pockets. Reeve MacGee was more than his sister's husband. As head of security, he would have some answers. And Bennett certainly had the questions—dozens of them. More was being done than the placing of extra guards. Bennett refused to go through the next weeks blindly while others worked to protect him and his family.

Swearing softly, he looked up at the sky. The moon was cloudless and half full. Another time, with the scents of the garden wafting around him, he would have itched for a woman to watch the sky with. Now, filled with frustration, he preferred the solitude.

When he heard the dogs bark, his body stiffened. He'd thought himself alone; he'd even been sure of it. In any case, his aging hounds never barked at family or familiar servants. Half-hoping for a confrontation, Bennett moved quietly toward the sound.

He heard her laugh and the sound surprised him. It wasn't quiet and prim, but rich and delighted. As he watched, Hannah leaned down to stroke the dogs, which pressed against her legs.

"There now, what a lovely pair you are." Smiling she bent farther still to nuzzle. The moonlight slanted over her face and throat.

Instantly, Bennett's eyes narrowed. She hardly looked plain and subdued at the moment. The moonlight accented the hollows and contours of her face, enriching the soft English skin and deepening the already deep green eyes. He would have sworn that he saw both strength and passion there. And he was a man who recognized both in a woman. Her laughter floated out again, as rich as sunlight, as sultry as fog.

"No, you mustn't jump," she cautioned the dogs as they circled her. "You'll have mud all over me and how would I explain that?"

"It's usually best not to explain at all."

She snapped her head up as Bennett spoke. He saw surprise, or thought he did, but it passed quickly. When she straightened, she was the calm, unremarkable Lady Hannah again. He chalked up the passion he'd thought he'd seen to a trick of the light.

"Good evening, Your Highness." Hannah took only a moment to curse herself for being caught unaware.

"I didn't know anyone else was in the garden."

"Nor did I." And she should have. "I beg your pardon."

"Don't." He smiled to put her at ease. "I've always felt the gardens aren't enjoyed nearly enough. Couldn't you sleep?"

"No, sir. I'm always restless when I travel." The dogs had deserted her for Bennett. She stood beside the flowering jasmine and watched him stroke them with strong, capable hands. She was well aware that numerous ladies had enjoyed the same easy touch. "I'd seen the gardens from my window and thought I might walk awhile." In truth, it had been their scent, exotic and alluring, that had urged her to loiter after she'd noted the layout of the space.

"I prefer them at night myself. Things often look different at night," he continued, studying her again. "Don't you think?"

"Naturally." She linked her hands together just below the waist. He was marvelous to look at, sun or moon. When he'd strode into his father's office that afternoon she'd thought that riding clothes suited him best. The dogs came back to press their noses against her joined hands.

"They like you."

"I've always been fond of animals." She unlinked her hands to stroke. He noticed for the first time that her hands were delicate, long and slender like her body. "What are their names?"

"Boris and Natasha."

"Suitable names for Russian wolfhounds."

"They were given to me as puppies. I named them after characters in an American cartoon show. Spies."

Her hands hesitated only a heartbeat. "Spies, Your Highness?"

"Inept Russian spies who were forever after a moose and squirrel."

He thought he saw it again, the flash of humor that lent something special to her face. "I see. I've never been to America."

"No?" He moved closer, but saw nothing but a young woman with good bones and a quiet manner. "It's a fascinating country. Cordina's become closely linked with it since two members of the Royal Family have married Americans."

"A fact that disappointed a number of hopeful Europeans, I'm sure." Hannah relaxed enough for a cautious smile. "I met Princess Gabriella several years ago. She's a beautiful woman."

"Yes, she is. You know, I've been to England several times. It's strange we never met."

Hannah allowed the smile to linger. "But we did, Your Highness."

"Boris, sit," Bennett commanded as the dog lifted a paw toward Hannah's dress. "Are you sure?"

"Quite sure, sir. Then you'd hardly be expected to remember. It was several years ago at a charity ball hosted by the Prince of Wales. The Queen Mother introduced you to me and my cousin Lady Sara. I believe you and Sara became . . . friendly.''

"Sara?" His mind backtracked and zeroed in. His memory, always good, was faultless when it came to women. "Yes, of course." Though he remembered Hannah only as a vague shadow beside her glamorous and bold cousin. "How is Sara?"

"Very well, sir." If there was sarcasm, it was well coated with manners. "Happily married for the second time. Shall I send her your regards?"

"If you like." He dipped his hands into his pockets again as he continued to study her. "You were wearing blue, a pale blue that was nearly white."

Hannah lifted her brow. She didn't have to be told that he'd barely noticed her. The fact that he hadn't, yet still remembered the color of her gown gave her a moment's pause. A memory like that could be useful—or dangerous.

"You flatter me, Your Highness."

"I make it a policy not to forget a woman."

"Yes, I can believe that."

"My reputation precedes me." The frown was there, then gone, to be replaced by a careless smile. "Does it concern you to be alone in the garden, in the moonlight with—"

"The Royal Rake?" Hannah finished.

"You do read," Bennett murmured.

"Incessantly. And no, Your Highness, I'm quite comfortable, thank you."

He opened his mouth, then laughed and shut it again. "Lady Hannah, I've rarely been put so neatly in my place."

So he was quick—another point she'd have to remember. "I beg your pardon, sir. That certainly wasn't my intention."

"The hell it wasn't, and well done." He took her hand and found it cool and steady. Perhaps she would prove to be a great deal less dull than he'd anticipated. "I should beg your pardon for baiting you, but I won't since you obviously hold your own so well. I'm beginning to see why Eve wanted you here."

Hannah had learned long ago to block off any form of guilt. She did so now. "I became very fond of her in a short time and was delighted with the opportunity to stay in Cordina for a few months. I confess, I've already fallen in love with little Princess Marissa."

"Barely a year old and she's already ruling the palace." Bennett's eyes softened as he thought of his brother's first child. "Maybe it's because she looks like Eve."

Hannah withdrew her hand from his. She'd heard the rumors that Bennett had been half in love, or possibly more than half in love, with his brother's wife. It didn't take even so talented an observer as she to hear the affection in his voice. She told herself to file it away. It may or may not have its uses later.

"If you'll excuse me, sir, I should go back to my room."

"It's still early." He found himself reluctant to let her go. It was unexpected that she would be easy to talk to, or that he would find himself needing to talk to her.

"I'm in the habit of retiring early."

"I'll walk you back."

"Please don't trouble. I know the way. Good night, Your Highness." She merged quickly with the shadows while the dogs whined a bit and thumped their tails against his legs.

What was there about her? Bennett wondered as he bent to soothe his pets. At first glance she seemed almost bland enough to fade into the wallpaper, and yet... He didn't know. But as he walked back toward the palace with the dogs at his heels, he resolved to find out. If nothing else, probing a bit beneath Lady Hannah's quiet breeding would keep his mind off Deboque.

Hannah didn't wait to see if he followed her, but walked quickly through the garden doors. She'd been born with the talent to move quietly, so unobtrusively she could easily be missed in a group of three people. It was a talent she'd honed to a skill and which served her well.

She moved up the stairs without a sound, never looking back. If you had to check whether you were being followed, you were already in trouble. Once inside her own room, she locked the door and slipped out of her practical pumps. Because the woman she professed to be would never leave her clothing scattered, Hannah picked them up, and with only a brief look of distaste, placed them neatly in her closet.

Checking only to see that her curtains were drawn, she peeled off the unflattering cocktail dress.

Although she thought it deserved its day in the garbage, she carefully hung it on a padded hanger.

She stood now, a slimly curved woman with milk-pale skin and long legs in a skimpy lace-edged teddy. Drawing the confining pins from her hair, she let it fall heavily to her waist with a sigh of pure pleasure.

Anyone who knew Lady Hannah Rothchild would have been stunned by the transformation, so complete, so ingrained was the role she'd played for nearly ten years.

Lady Hannah had a passion for silk and Breton lace, but confined it to nightwear and lingerie. Linens and tweeds were more fitting to the image she'd worked hard to create.

Lady Hannah enjoyed reading a pot-boiling thriller in a steamy bubble bath, but she kept a copy of Chaucer on her nightstand and if asked, could quote and discuss a handful of obscure passages.

It wasn't a matter of split personality, but necessity. If she'd given it any deep thought, Hannah would have been able to state that she was comfortable with both of her selves. In fact, more often than not she thoroughly liked the plain, polite and marginally pretty Hannah. Otherwise, she could never have tolerated the sensible shoes for extended periods.

But there was another part to Lady Hannah Rothchild, only daughter of Lord Rothchild, granddaughter of the Earl of Fenton. That part was not quiet and unassuming, but shrewd and sometimes reckless. More, that part had a taste for danger and a mind that absorbed and stored the most minor detail.

Combined, those parts of Lady Hannah Rothchild equaled an excellent and highly skilled agent.

Ignoring her robe, Hannah opened her top drawer and drew out a long, locked box. Inside was a strand of pearls handed down from her great-grandmother with matching earrings her father had had reset for her twenty-first birthday. In the drawers of the box were several other pieces of jewelry befitting a young woman of her class.

Hannah pulled a notebook out of the false bottom and taking it to the rosewood writing desk, began to write her daily report. She hadn't gone into the garden merely to smell the roses, though she had lingered too long because of them. Now she had the complete layout and no longer had to rely on the information fed her. She took the time to draw a sketch of the palace, including the doors and windows most easily accessible. By the following day, or the day after at most, she would have a schedule of the guards.

It had taken her little time to form a friendship with Eve. Securing an invitation to the palace in Cordina had been as easy as asking for one. Eve missed her sister and the familiarity of her own country. She'd needed a friend, one she could talk to, one who would share her delight in her daughter.

Hannah had obliged.

She felt the quick trickle of guilt again and ignored it. A job was a job, she reminded herself. She couldn't let the fondness she felt for Eve interfere with a goal she'd begun to work toward two years ago.

With a shake of her head, she made her first notes on Bennett. He wasn't completely what she'd expected, Hannah thought now. Oh, he was as charming and as attractive as his dossier had said, but he'd given the dull Lady Hannah his time and attention.

An egotistical womanizer, Hannah reminded herself. That had been her own conclusion after doing her research on him. Perhaps he was a bit bored and entertained thoughts of distracting himself with a vulnerable and accessible woman.

Narrowing her eyes, Hannah looked back on the way he had smiled at her. A man of his looks, position and experience knew how to use that smile or a soft word to enchant a woman of any age and any class. The fact that he'd done so, with astonishing regularity, was well documented. Perhaps he would try to add another jewel to his crown by seducing her.

She remembered the way he'd looked in the moonlight, the way his eyes had warmed when she'd bantered back with him. His hand had been firm and hard when it had taken hers—the hand of a man who did more than wave regally to his people.

With a shake of her head, she brought herself up short. It wouldn't do to consider a dalliance with Bennett for enjoyment, but for its usefulness. Thoughtfully, she tapped her pencil on the pad. No, a romance with Bennett would only lead to complications, no matter how advantageous it might be in the long run. She'd keep her eyes down and her hands folded.

Carefully, Hannah hid the notebook again and replaced the false bottom. The box was locked, but left in full sight if anyone searched her dresser.

She was in, she told herself with a growing sense of anticipation as she looked around the room.

When Deboque walked out of prison in two days' time, he'd be very pleased.

Chapter Two

"Oh, Hannah, I'm so glad you agreed to visit awhile." With her arm hooked with her new friend's, Eve strolled behind the backdrop at the theater. Her body remained slender during the early months of her pregnancy, but her dress was cleverly cut to conceal even the slight weight gain. "Alex doesn't find it as necessary to pamper me to death now that you're here. He finds you so sensible."

"I am sensible."

Eve's low chuckle flowed into her easy Texas drawl. "I know, that's the beauty of it, but you're not always telling me to sit down and put my feet up."

"Men sometimes look at pregnancy and childbirth as a traumatic disease rather than a fact of life."

"That's it exactly." Delighted with Hannah's dry wit, Eve drew her into her office. With Gabriella so often in America and her own sister visiting only rarely, Eve had indeed yearned for another woman to relax with. "Alex keeps expecting me to faint or get overly emotional. I never felt better in my life, except perhaps when I was carrying Marissa."

Tossing back her fall of dark hair, Eve perched on the edge of her desk. Here, at least, she could still claim some measure of the privacy she'd given up when she'd married a prince. Though she never regretted the sacrifice, she always enjoyed stealing a bit of her own back.

"If you hadn't come, I'd have had to fight him tooth and nail to continue working. He only agreed because he felt you'd keep a close eye on me when he's busy."

"Then I won't disappoint him." Hannah took quick stock of the office. No window, no outside access. With a smile, she chose a chair. "You know, Eve, I really admire you. The Fine Arts Center always had a good reputation but since you took over here, this theater has become one of the most important in Europe."

"It's what I've always wanted." Eve looked down at the diamond-encrusted band on her finger. Even after two years it sometimes astonished her to find it there. "You know, Hannah, some mornings I'm almost afraid to wake up; I think that I'll find out it was all a dream. Then I look at Alex and Marissa and think, they're mine. Really mine." Her eyes clouded a moment with both fear and determination. "I won't let anything or anyone hurt them."

"No one will." Eve's thoughts were on Deboque, Hannah surmised. The princess was bound by duty to keep some fears to herself. "Now, not to pamper, but I think we could both use some tea, then you can show me what sort of job I can do around here."

Eve brought herself back with an effort. Nightmares of Deboque, a man she'd never seen, continued to plague her. "Tea's a wonderful idea, but I didn't bring you to the Center to work. I just thought you'd like to see it."

"Eve, you of all people should understand that I need something to do or I'll be bored to death."

"But I'd hoped this could be a vacation for you."

The guilt shimmered a bit. "Some people aren't meant for vacations."

"All right then. Why don't you watch rehearsals with me for an hour or two and give me an honest opinion?"

"I'd love to."

"Great. I'm worried about the opening. We only have a couple of weeks left and I've had nothing but trouble with this playwright."

"Oh, who is it?"

Eve rose and took a deep breath. "Me."

* * *

Hannah drank her tea and stayed in the background. It didn't take long for her to see that Eve was respected not only as the wife of the heir, but for her knowledge of theater. She noted too that guards, unobtrusive but in force, were always close at hand. When the princess was in the theater, every entrance was blocked, every interior door was double guarded. Hannah was also aware that a special unit of security checked the Center daily for explosives.

While seated mid-theater with Eve, Hannah watched the rehearsal. She'd always had an affection and respect for actors, as she understood the effort and skill that went into characterization. Now, while lines were cued and staging set, she matched the members of the troupe with the information she already had compiled on each of them.

They were certainly talented, Hannah thought as she found herself drawn into the rhythm and emotion of Eve's play. The sets were still incomplete, but the players needed no more than Eve's words and their own skill to make a statement. Each one of the actors had a reputation in theater and a complete security check.

But it had been an actor—Russ Talbot—who'd nearly carried out Deboque's revenge two years before. Hannah couldn't forget that it was a strong possibility that someone other than herself had been planted. Deboque was known for covering his bets.

"She's wonderful, isn't she?"

Drawn back, Hannah looked over at Eve. "I beg your pardon?"

"Chantel O'Hurley. She's exquisite." Shifting in her chair, Eve leaned on the seat back in front of her. "She rarely makes a stage performance, so we're lucky to have her. I'm sure you've seen her films in England."

"Yes." Hannah gave her full attention to the curvy blonde center stage.

Chantel O'Hurley. Hannah paused to recollect everything she'd read in the actress's file. Twenty-six. American film star. Residence, Beverly Hills. Daughter of Frances and Margaret O'Hurley, traveling entertainers. Sisters, Abigail and Madelaine. Brother, Trace.

Hannah frowned and continued to watch. She had full background information on the entire O'Hurley family, except the brother. There her sources had closed tight. In any case, Chantel O'Hurley was a talented actress with an impressive list of screen credits and no known affiliation with any political group. Nonetheless, Hannah would keep an eye on her.

"She's found the heart of it," Eve murmured. "I'd finished the play and was trying to work up the courage to produce it, when I saw her in her last film. I knew immediately she'd be the perfect Julia." On a long breath Eve leaned back again in an unprincesslike slouch. "I can't believe she's here, reciting my lines. There isn't an emotion that voice can't pull out."

"I'm sure she's honored to be performing in a play written and produced by Princess Eve of Cordina."

On a half laugh, Eve shook her head. "If the play had been lousy, I could have been Empress of Europe and Chantel wouldn't have accepted the part. That's what I'm hanging onto."

"A member of the Royal Family doesn't write lousy plays."

At the sound of the voice behind her, Eve was springing up and reaching out. "Alexander! What are you doing here?"

"I, too, have an interest in the Center." He kissed the hand he held before turning to Hannah. "Please, sit, I didn't mean to disturb you."

"No." Eve sighed and glanced back at the stage where rehearsals continued. "You meant to check up on me."

It was, of course, the truth, but Alexander only shrugged. In the dim light, Hannah saw his gaze sweep over his wife's head to the guards placed at several strategic points. "You forget, *ma mie*, that I am still president of the Center. In addition to that, my wife's play is in rehearsal. I have a small interest there as well."

"And you came to be certain I wasn't staying on my feet." Over the frustration came the tug of love. Eve rose to her toes to kiss him. "Thank you. Hannah, tell His Highness I've been taking care of myself in the four hours and forty minutes since he last saw me."

"Your Highness," Hannah began dutifully, "the princess has been taking excellent care of herself."

A smile softened his features, but he continued to stand protectively near his wife. "Thank you, Hannah. I'm sure the credit goes to you."

With a low laugh, Eve tucked her hand through Alexander's arm. "Hannah, you can see that I wasn't joking when I said that Alex thinks I need a keeper. If you hadn't come I have no doubt he'd have hired a two-hundred-pound wrestler with tattoos."

"I'm glad I could save you from that." What was this? Hannah wondered. A tug of envy? Ridiculous as it seemed to her, she recognized the emotion as she studied Alexander and Eve. So much in love, she thought. The power of it all but cast an aura around them. Did they realize, could they realize, how rare a thing they'd found?

"Now that I've interrupted," Alexander was saying, "I was hoping to convince you to join me for my luncheon with the American senator."

"The Yankee from Maine."

With a smile, Alexander stroked her cheek. "My dear, it continues to fascinate me how your country divides itself into sections. But yes, the Yankee from Maine. We should be finished by three and be back at the palace when Marissa wakes from her nap."

"But you had a meeting this afternoon."

"I canceled it." He brought her hand to his lips. "I wanted to spend some time with my family."

The glow of pleasure all but lit up the theater. "Give me five minutes to get my things. Hannah, you'll join us?"

"If it wouldn't inconvenience you, I'd really like to stay and watch the rest of the rehearsal." Her mind was already shooting ahead. Alone, she could take a casual tour of the complex. If there were vulnerabilities, she'd find them.

"Of course, stay as long as you like." Eve bent down to kiss her cheek. "We'll have a car wait for you at the stage door. Five minutes," she repeated to Alexander before she dashed off.

"What do you think of the play?" Alexander asked Hannah as he took the seat beside her.

"I'm hardly an expert on the theater, Your Highness."

"In private, please call me Alexander."

"Thank you," she murmured, aware that this gave her an intimacy awarded to few. "There's an intensity, an immediacy in the dialogue that makes one care deeply about the characters. I don't know the end, but I find myself hoping Julia wins even while I'm afraid she won't."

"Eve would like to hear that. The play—and other things—have her very tense right now."

"You're worried about her." In a gesture that was pure instinct, Hannah placed a hand on his. "She's very strong."

"I know that, better than most." But he'd never been able to block off the memory of how her body had stiffened, then gone limp in his arms when a bullet had struck her. "I haven't told you before how very grateful I am that you came to be with her. She needs friendship. I changed her life, selfishly perhaps because I couldn't live mine without her. Whatever can be done to give her a sense of normalcy, a sense of peace, I'll do. You understand the obligations of royalty. The limitations. Even the risks.''

"Yes, I do." Hannah left her hand on his another moment before removing it. "And I understand a happy woman when I see one."

When he turned to her then, Hannah saw the strong resemblance to his father. The lean, almost scholarly face, the aristocratic lines, the mouth that was held firm. "Thank you, Hannah. I think perhaps you'll be good for all of us."

"I hope so." She looked back at the stage, at the players, at the roles. "I do hope so."

Alone, Hannah watched for another half hour. Yes, the play was good, she decided, even gripping, but she had other games to play.

The guards remained, but with no royalty present they were more for the purpose of keeping others out than monitoring those already in. Lady Hannah was already established as the princess's confidante and companion. Trusted by Prince Armand himself, she wasn't followed when she rose and slipped through a side door.

There was a miniature camera concealed in a lipstick case in her handbag, but she didn't use it now. Her training had taught her to rely on her powers of observation first, her equipment second.

A building the size of the sprawling Center wasn't easily secured. Hannah found herself giving Reeve MacGee a nod of respect as she walked through. Heat sensors as well as hidden cameras. But the sensors were activated only when the Center was closed.

Security passes were required at the door for members of the cast and crew. On the night of a performance, however, entrance could be gained for the price of a ticket. Deboque would step from behind bars in a day's time.

As she walked, leaving one corridor for the next, Hannah drew a blueprint in her mind. She'd studied the layout of the Center on paper before, but preferred to walk in it, to focus on it, to touch the walls and floor.

Too many blind corners, she thought. Too many small rooms used for storage. Too many places to hide. Even with Reeve's expertise, the building could be vulnerable with the right plan of attack. But then, Hannah believed any building could be.

She turned into Wardrobe, pretending a casual interest in the costumes. Did the guard at the door know everyone by sight? How easy would it be to replace one of the technicians? A photo was affixed to the pass, but makeup and hairpieces could take care of that. How often had she, or another like her, gained access to a place by faked credentials or a clever disguise?

Once inside, a man could disappear easily. If a man on the security panel could be bribed or replaced, so much the better.

Yes, she'd put that scenario in her report and let her superiors chew on it awhile. She'd add to that the fact that no one had checked her bag. A small plastic explosive could be easily carried and easily planted.

She walked from Wardrobe into a rehearsal hall walled with mirrors. With a little shock, she stared at her reflection on all sides. Then, as she had in the garden, she let out a low, easy laugh.

Oh, Hannah, she thought, how miserably dull you are. Turning to the side, she shook her head. No, maroon did nothing for her, and the high-necked jacket with its bulky belt only made her look unattractively thin. The skirt came well below the knee to hide her legs. She'd braided her hair today, tightly, then had circled the braid at the base of her neck.

Being a part of herself, it was the best cover she could have conceived. She'd been too skinny as a child, with unmanageable hair, and knees that were forever scraped. Her facial bones had been prominent even then, but in the young girl's face had seemed too sharp, too angular.

Then when the other girls had begun to bloom and curve, Hannah's body had remained stubbornly straight. She'd been bright and athletic and cheerful. Boys had patted her on the back and called her a good sport, but they hadn't been interested in taking her to any dances.

She'd learned to ride, swim, shoot skeet and to put an arrow in a bull's eye from a hundred paces, but she hadn't dated.

She'd learned to speak Russian and French and enough Cantonese to surprise even her father, but she'd gone alone to her own graduation ball.

When she turned twenty, her body changed, but Hannah hid the late blossoming under dull clothes. She'd already chosen her path in life. Beauty turned heads and in her field it was always best to go unnoticed.

Now, she looked at the results in the wall of mirrors and was satisfied. No man would desire her. It was human nature to look at the physical shell and draw emotion from that long before you dipped beneath to the intellect or soul. No woman would envy her. Dull was safe, after all.

No one would suspect a plain, bookish woman of excellent breeding and quiet social manners of deception or violence. Only a select few were aware that the woman beneath was capable of both.

For a reason she couldn't name, that thought made her turn away from her reflection. Deception had been with her all of her adult life, and yet she couldn't quite dismiss the twinges of guilt she felt whenever Eve looked at her as a friend.

It was a job, Hannah reminded herself. No emotional attachments, no emotional involvements were permitted. That was the first and most important rule of the game. She couldn't afford to allow herself to like Eve, to even think of her as anything but a political symbol. If she did, everything she'd worked for could be lost.

The envy had to go as well, Hannah reminded herself. It was a dangerous lapse to let herself look at the love between the prince and Eve and wish something similar for herself. There was no room for love in her profession. There were only goals, commitments and risks.

There would be no prince for her, royal or otherwise.

But before she could prevent it, her thoughts turned to Bennett and the way he'd smiled at her in the moonlight.

Idiot, she told herself and began tightening a few loose pins. He was the last person she should think about in a personal way. If for no other reason, there was his dossier and the astonishing list of women who'd been part of his life already.

Use him, certainly, her mind went on. But don't think about him as anything but a means to an end. Romantic fantasies had ended for her at sixteen. Ten years later, in the middle of her most important job, was hardly the time to begin to weave them again. She would do well to remember that the stiff-lipped, proper Lady Hannah would never see His Royal Highness Prince Bennett de Cordina in a romantic light.

But the woman within dreamed and for a moment strained against the confines she'd built herself.

Hannah turned to look back at the mirrors when she heard the footsteps.

Immediately alert, she cast her eyes down and walked from the room.

"Ah, there you are."

At Bennett's voice, Hannah gave an inward curse, but curtsied. "Your Highness."

"Taking the grand tour?" He walked closer, wondering why she looked as plain as a maiden aunt and continued to intrigue him.

"Yes, sir. I hope it's all right."

"Of course." He took her hand, willing her to look directly at him. There was something about her eyes.... Or perhaps it was her voice, that cool, always composed British tone. "I had some business in town. Alexander suggested I swing by when I'd finished to see if you were ready to go back."

"That's very kind of you." And oh, how she would have preferred a silent, anonymous driver who'd have given her the opportunity to assimilate her report on the drive back.

"I was here." He felt the restlessness layer over him as she drew her hand back to her side. "If you'd like to see more, I'd be happy to take you around the rest of the Center."

Hannah weighed the pros and cons in a matter of seconds. Another quick look might add something, but she'd already gone through the main theater twice, once with Eve and once alone. It might begin to look odd if she went through again with Bennett.

"No, thank you. It is a fascinating place. I've never seen a theater from this side."

"Eve's territory. I confess I prefer front row center myself." He took Hannah's arm and began to lead her down the hall. "If you hang around her for any length of time, she finds something for you to do. With me, it's usually moving boxes. Heavy boxes."

With a laugh, Hannah slanted him a look. "That's one of the best uses a woman can find for a man."

"I can see why Eve took to you." He'd come simply to do his sister-in-law a favor, but now found himself glad. Outward appearance aside, Lady Hannah was anything but dull. For perhaps the first time in his life, Bennett was beginning to look beneath the physical. "Have you seen much of Cordina yet, Hannah?"

She noticed he'd dropped her title, but decided to let it pass. "Only snatches so far, sir. Once I'm a bit more familiar with Eve's routine, I plan to explore a bit. I've heard your museum has some excellent exhibits. The building itself is reported to be a fine example of post-Renaissance architecture."

He wasn't interested in exhibits, but in her. "Do you like the water?"

"Of course. Sea air is very beneficial for the constitution."

With a half laugh, Bennett paused at the top of the stairs. "But do you like it?"

He had a strange talent for looking at a woman as though he were seeing her for the first time. And looking as though it mattered. Despite her training, Hannah felt her pulse rate accelerate. "Yes. My grandmother has a place near Cornwall. I spent several summers there as a girl."

He wondered what she would look like with her hair down and the sea wind teasing it. Would she laugh as he had heard her laugh in the garden? Would he see that light flash in her eyes again? Then he realized it didn't matter how she looked. He went on impulse, knowing he might regret it.

"I have to go into Le Havre in a couple of days. The drive runs along the coast. Come with me."

If he'd asked her to step into the storage room and neck, she would have been no less surprised. Surprise turned quickly to caution and caution to calculation. But beneath it all was the simple pleasure that he wanted her company. It was the pleasure that worried her.

"It's kind of you to ask, Your Highness, but Eve may have plans."

"Then we'll check with her first." He wanted her to go. He found himself already looking forward to spending a few hours with her away from the palace. Perhaps it was for the challenge of it, the challenge of picking away at that prim, proper exterior and finding what, if anything, lay beneath. Whatever the reason was, Bennett didn't question it. "Would you like to go?"

"Yes, I would." Hannah told herself it was because it would give her the opportunity to study him more closely, for professional reasons. She told herself it would give her the chance to see how well security worked away from the palace and the capital. But the truth was as simple as her answer. She wanted to go.

"Fine, then we'll fix it, and you can stand through the long and wordy welcoming ceremony with me."

"Hate to be bored alone, do you?"

Laughing, Bennett took her hand again. "Yes, I can see exactly why Eve brought you to us." Her hand was an inch from his lips when the murmur of voices came from below. Glancing down, more than a little annoyed, Bennett spotted Chantel.

"The anger has to show," she was insisting, walking so quickly the director had to lengthen his stride to keep up. "Julia is not a passive woman. She doesn't hide what she feels no matter what the consequences. Dammit, Maurice, I'll make it subtle. I know my job."

"Of course you do, *chérie*, that I don't question. It is simply that—"

"*Mademoiselle.*" From the top of the stairs, Bennett looked down. Hannah had a firsthand glimpse of how he smiled at a truly beautiful woman. Without thinking, she drew her hand from his and linked her fingers together.

Chantel, reaching one hand up to draw back her pale blond hair, tilted her head back. Even so dispassionate an observer such as Hannah had to concede that few women could claim such a combination of glamour, beauty and sexuality. Her lips curved. Her eyes, a deep, dreamy shade of blue, smiled with them.

"Your Highness," Chantel said in her rich, smoky voice as she dipped into a formal curtsy. She started up the stairs and Bennett started down. In the middle, they stopped, then Chantel reached up to touch his face before bringing him closer for a lengthy kiss. Above them, Hannah felt her teeth snap together. "It's been a long time."

"Too long." Bennett cupped her hand in both of his. "You're lovelier than ever. It's astonishing."

"It's genes," Chantel claimed, and grinned at him. "My God, Bennett, what a beautiful man you are. If I wasn't a cynic, I'd propose."

"If I wasn't terrified of you, I'd accept." They embraced again with the ease of old friends. "Chantel, it's good to see you again. Eve was turning handsprings when you agreed to take the part."

"It's a good play." Chantel gave a matter-of-fact shrug. "Even though I adore you, I wouldn't have come all this way to take a role in a bomb. Your sister-in-law's a talented woman." Chantel cast a look over her shoulder at the director waiting respectfully at the bottom of the stairs. "You might mention to her that I'm fighting to preserve the integrity of her Julia." As she turned back, she spotted Hannah standing on the landing. "Friend of yours?"

Glancing back, Bennett held out a hand. "Hannah, come meet the incomparable Chantel."

The stiffness in her movement only suited her character, Hannah told herself as she started down. All unremarkable women tensed up when slapped in the face with great beauty. She stopped on the step beside Bennett, but kept nearly a foot of space between them.

"Lady Hannah Rothchild, Chantel O'Hurley."

"How do you do?" Formal and proper, Hannah held out a hand. Chantel kept her face passive as she accepted it.

"I do fine, thank you." As a woman, as an actress who understood angles and role-playing, she wondered why someone with such good bone structure and a flawless complexion would deliberately make themselves appear plain.

"Lady Hannah is keeping Eve company for a few months."

"How nice. Cordina's a beautiful country. I'm sure you'll enjoy it."

"Yes, I already am. I also enjoyed watching you rehearse."

"Thanks, but we have a way to go." Chantel tapped a finger on the banister and wondered why she felt such instant distrust. Dismissing it as overwork, she turned back to Bennett. "I have to run. Try to make some time for me, darling."

"Of course. You're coming to dinner Saturday with the rest of the cast?"

"Wouldn't miss it. I'll see you there, Lady Hannah."

"Goodbye, Miss O'Hurley."

After giving Bennett a quick pat on the cheek, Chantel descended the stairs again and let the director trail behind her.

"She's quite a woman," Bennett murmured.

"Yes, she's very beautiful."

"There's that, too." Without looking at her, Bennett took Hannah's arm again. "I suppose I've always admired her willpower and ambition. She's determined to be the best and isn't afraid to work for it. Every time I see her on the screen, it's breathtaking."

Hannah dug her fingers into her purse and reminded herself she was supposed to be unassuming. "You admire ambition, Your Highness?"

"Nothing's changed for better or worse without it."

"Some men still find ambition in a woman unflattering, or at least, uncomfortable."

"Some men are idiots."

"I couldn't agree more," Hannah said dryly, dryly enough that he lifted his brow as he gazed at her.

"Why am I never quite sure whether or not you're insulting me, Hannah?"

"I beg your pardon, sir, I was simply agreeing with you."

He stopped again. From the stage came the murmur of voices, but the hall was deserted. Bennett took her chin in his hand, ignoring her jolt of shock, and studied her face. "Hannah, why is it when I look at you I'm not convinced I'm seeing all there is?"

Alarm bells went off in her head. Her face paled a bit. She knew it, but thought, hoped, he would take that as natural. Not by another blink did she show concern. "I don't know what you mean."

"I wonder." He moved his thumb over her jawline, then just beneath where the skin was softer yet, and warm. "Yes, I wonder more than I should about you, Hannah. Do you have an answer for that?"

There were amber flecks in his eyes, turning what might have been plain brown into something tawny and compelling. He had the mouth of a poet and the hands of a farmer. Hannah wondered how it was possible to combine the two as her heart, always so steady, began to drum against her ribs.

"Your Highness—" It was both the lady without and the lady within who fumbled.

"Do you, Hannah?"

He saw her lips part. Strange, he hadn't noticed how attractive her mouth was before—soft, just a bit wide and beautifully shaped without cosmetics. He wondered if it would taste as cool as her voice or as rich as her eyes.

She had to stop this, here and now. The yearning building inside her could only be destructive. Even as she longed to reach out, she cast her eyes down. "No, sir, except that many times men are intrigued with a woman simply because she's not what they're accustomed to."

"We'll see." He backed off, though the effort it cost him was a surprise. "I'll take you back now, Hannah, and we'll both give it some thought."

Chapter Three

Hannah was given free run of the palace and the grounds. She had only to ask and her bath would be drawn or her bed turned down. If she developed a craving for hot chocolate at three a.m., she could pick up the phone beside her bed and request it. As a guest of the Royal Family, she was afforded every amenity the palace could offer.

And as a guest of the Royal Family, she was afforded her own guards.

Hannah considered them only a slight nuisance. It was a simple enough matter for someone of her talents to make them think she was tucked safely away in her rooms while she was somewhere else entirely. However, the fact that she was being watched made it difficult to set up a meeting with her contact on the outside.

Using the palace phones was out of the question. Too many extensions made it a risk that even a casual, coded conversation could be overheard. She'd briefly considered smuggling in a transmitter, then had rejected the notion. Transmissions could be traced. She hadn't spent two years of her life to get to this point to see it all wiped away because of some electronic foul-up. In any case, she preferred meetings of such importance to be face-to-face.

Two days after she arrived in Cordina, she mailed a letter. It was addressed to an old family friend in Sussex who didn't exist. Its destination was one of Deboque's many branches throughout Europe. If for any reason the letter was intercepted and opened, the reader would find nothing more interesting than a chatty note describing Cordina and the weather.

Once the letter reached its destination and was decoded, it would read differently. Hannah had given her name, her rank in the organization and had requested a meeting, detailing the time, date and place. The information would be fed back to the Cordina contact. All she had to do was get there, alone.

One week, Hannah thought once the letter was on its way. In one week she would well and truly begin what had been started so long ago. She had plenty to do to keep her busy in the meantime.

Princess Gabriella and her family were visiting the palace that evening. The staff had been in an uproar for the better part of the day, more, Hannah guessed, because the children were descending than for any other reason. Hannah had heard that the priceless collection of Fabergé eggs was to be put out of reach.

She spent the day quietly enough, visiting Eve and Marissa in the nursery, lunching with several members of the Historical Society, and in the lull of late afternoon, exploring the cellars for vulnerabilities.

Now, she clipped on her pearls and prepared to join the family in the main drawing room. It would be interesting to see them all together, she thought. In that way she could judge the interactions as well as the individuals. Before too much time had passed, she had to know them all as well as she knew herself. One mistake, one bad judgment call, and all could be lost.

"Come back here, you little demon!"

Hannah heard a loud laugh, a thud, then rushing feet. Before she had a chance to open the door to see for herself, it burst open. Barreling through it was a small boy with a thatch of dark hair that may or may not have been combed in the last week. He gave her an amazing grin, showing more than one gap before he scooted under her bed.

"Cachez-moi, s'il vous plaît!" His voice was muffled by the skirt of the spread before he disappeared.

Hannah opened her mouth again only to see Bennett filling the doorway.

"Did you see a small, miserably mannered boy?"

"I, ah—No," she decided on the spot and folded her hands. "I did think I heard someone go running past. What are you—"

"Thanks. If you see him, lock him in a closet or something." He started off down the hall. "Dorian, you nasty little thief, you can't hide forever."

Hannah walked to the door and looked out to see Bennett turning the corner before she closed it. Moving back to the bed, she crouched down and lifted the skirt. "I think it's safe now," Hannah told him in French.

The dark hair poked out first, then a sturdy little body dressed in short pants and a white linen shirt that were streaked with dirt. If Hannah hadn't already seen his picture, she would have taken him for one of the servants' offspring. But he was royal.

"You are English. I speak excellent English."

"So you do."

"Thank you for hiding me from my uncle." Young Prince Dorian bowed. Though he wasn't yet five, he executed it perfectly. "He was angry, but he doesn't stay that way long. I'm Prince Dorian."

"Your Highness." Hannah curtsied. "It's a pleasure to meet you. I'm Lady Hannah Rothchild." Then unable to resist, she bent down to his level. "What did you steal?"

Dorian glanced at the closed door, back at Hannah, then grinned. Digging into his back pocket he pulled out a yo-yo. It might once have been blue, but now it was the gray of old wood with a few chips of brighter paint still holding. Hannah studied it with appropriate respect.

"This is Bennett's—His Highness's?" Hannah corrected.

"*Merveilleux, n'est-ce pas?* He's had it since he was five." Dorian turned the toy over in his hand, marveling that it had once been new and shiny when his uncle had been just the age he was now. "He gets angry when I go into his room and play with it, but how else am I going to be able to make it work?"

"Good point." Hannah barely resisted the urge to ruffle the royal head of hair. "And one would doubt he plays with it himself very often."

"He keeps it on a shelf. It isn't that he really minds me looking at it," Dorian explained, loyal to the core. "It's just that when I try to make it work, the string gets all tangled and knotted up."

"It takes a little practice."

"I know." He grinned again. "And I can only practice if I steal it."

"Your logic is flawless, Your Highness. May I see?"

Dorian hesitated only a moment, then graciously handed it over. "Girls usually aren't interested in such things." He made a grimace of masculine disgust. "My sisters play with dolls."

"Everyone has different tastes, I suppose." Hannah slid her finger into the loop, wondering how long it had been since Bennett's had fit there. The string wasn't as old as the toy itself. By her guess, it would have been replaced more than a dozen times over the years. On impulse, she let the yo-yo slide down, dangle, then brought it neatly up.

"Oh, nicely done." Charmed, Dorian watched her with wide eyes.

"Thank you, sir. I used to have one of my own. It was red," she remembered with a half smile. "Until my dog chewed it up."

"Can you do any tricks? I tried Round The World once and broke a lamp. Uncle Bennett scolded me, but then he tossed out the pieces himself so no one would know."

Because she could picture it so well, Hannah smiled. A loud roar, but little bite, she decided and wished she didn't like him the better for it. "A trick?" As she considered she took the yo-yo up and down. Then, with a quick flick of her wrist took it Round The World. When it snapped back in her palm, Dorian laughed and climbed on her bed.

"Do another, please."

Calling on memory, Hannah Walked the Dog and had the young prince bouncing on the bed and calling out for more.

"Well done, Lady Hannah," Bennett said from the doorway. "Obviously you have hidden talents."

Hannah had to bite off an oath as she brought the yo-yo back. "Your Highness." Toy in hand, she curtsied. "I didn't hear you knock."

"I didn't." Bennett pushed away from the doorjamb he was leaning on to walk to the bed. Unrepentant, his nephew grinned up at him.

"Isn't she wonderful, Uncle Bennett?"

"We'll discuss the Lady Hannah's attributes later." He gave Dorian's ear a twist before turning around. "My property, if you will."

Fighting to keep a straight face, Hannah handed it to him.

"This might seem to be nothing more than a simple child's toy," Bennett began as he slipped it into his pocket. "But in fact, it's an heirloom."

"I see." She cleared her throat on the laugh, but it escaped anyway. Hoping she looked contrite, she stared at the floor. "I beg your pardon, sir."

"The hell you do. And he was in here all along wasn't he?" Bennett pushed his nephew flat on the bed and sent him into a fit of giggles. "You let me go running off all over the palace looking for this petty thief when all the time he was hiding behind your skirts."

"The bed skirts to be honest, sir." She had to clear her throat again, but managed to speak calmly. "When you rushed by with so vague a description, I had no idea you were looking for Prince Dorian."

"I admire a good liar," Bennett murmured as he moved closer. For the second time he caught her chin in his hand. But for the first time, she saw all of the arrogance he was capable of and felt all of its attraction. "And I grow only more intrigued."

"Lady Hannah can do a double Round the World."

"Fascinating." Bennett slid his hand away slowly as he turned back to his nephew. If he'd listened for it, he might have heard Hannah's slow sigh of relief. "I thought we had an agreement, Dorian."

Dorian's head drooped, but Hannah didn't notice that the light in his eyes dimmed in the least. "I only wanted to see it. I'm sorry, Uncle Bennett."

"Sure you are." Bennett hauled him up by the armpits, scowled, then kissed him soundly. "Your mother's downstairs. Don't slide in the halls on the way to the drawing room."

"All right." On his feet again, Dorian bowed to Hannah. "It was a pleasure meeting you, Lady Hannah."

"And you, sir."

He sent her a gap-toothed grin before he dashed off.

"Sweet talker," Bennett muttered. "Oh, you might think he's all charm, but he has a black heart."

"Strangely enough I was reminded of you."

With one brow lifted, Bennett rocked back on his heels. "Indeed, my lady, that is strange."

"He's a scoundrel, without question. And you love him."

"That's beside the point." Bennett stuck his hand in his pocket. "As to the matter of the yo-yo."

"Yes, sir?"

"Try to wait until I'm five feet away before you laugh in my face."

"As you wish, Your Highness."

"It was a gift from my mother when I was ill one summer. I've bought the little devil a dozen of them, but he keeps stealing mine. He knows if I don't get a son of my own by the time he's ten I'll make him a gift of it."

"I have a red-headed doll my mother gave me when I broke my wrist in a fall. I kept it when I outgrew all the others."

It wasn't until he'd taken her hand that she realized she'd told him something he didn't need to know, something she'd never told anyone else. Even as she warned herself such lapses were dangerous, his lips brushed her fingers.

"You, Lady Hannah, have a kind heart as well as a clever tongue. Come, walk downstairs with me and meet the rest of my family."

Reeve MacGee would be a formidable obstacle. Hannah had thought so before, but seeing him with his family, she was sure of it. She knew his background from the time he'd entered the police force as a rookie through his less publicized work for the United States government.

His involvement with Cordina and the Royal Family had the ring of romance, but Reeve was no poet. He'd come out of a self-imposed retirement at Prince Armand's request when Gabriella had been kidnapped. Though she'd escaped, her time in captivity had left its mark. Amnesia had plagued her and Reeve had been enlisted to protect her, and to investigate.

There had been no doubt that Deboque had been pushing the buttons, but though his lover had been captured and imprisoned, she'd never implicated him. Like other powerful men, Deboque inspired loyalty. Or fear.

During the time that Gabriella was struggling to regain her memory, she and Reeve had fallen in love. Although Reeve had refused to accept a title when they married, he'd agreed to head security in Cordina. Even with Reeve's experience and skill, the palace had been infiltrated once again.

Two years ago, Alexander had nearly been assassinated. Since that time, Reeve had managed to block any and all attempts on members of the Royal Family. But Deboque was about to walk out of prison. With freedom would come more power.

Hannah watched Reeve now, seeing a quiet, introspective man who plainly adored his wife and children. He would use everything available to protect them from harm. So much the better.

With her hands folded and her skirts smoothed, Hannah sat and listened.

"We all know your play's going to be a wonderful success." Gabriella, with her hand caught loosely in Reeve's, smiled at Eve. Her rich red hair was styled with casual chic around a face that remained delicate and lovely. "That doesn't mean we don't understand you have to worry about it."

"I'm at the point now where I wish it was over." Eve drew Marissa into her lap.

"But you're feeling well?"

"I'm feeling fine." Eve let Marissa climb down again. "Between Alex's pampering and Hannah's eagle eye, I can hardly lift a finger without a doctor's certificate."

"It's so good of you to come." Gabriella smiled at Hannah before she sipped some sparkling water. "I know firsthand how comforting it is to have a friend nearby. Are we keeping you happy enough so that you're not homesick?"

"I'm very happy in Cordina." Hannah kept her back straight against the sofa.

"I hope you'll come out to the farm while you're here."

"I've heard a great deal about it." Gabriella had been kidnapped there while it had still been an overgrown plot of land. "I'd love to see it for myself."

"Then we'll arrange it." Reeve spoke quietly as he lit a cigarette. "You're enjoying your visit so far?"

"Yes, I am." Their eyes met and held. "Cordina is a fascinating country. It has a fairy-tale aura perhaps, but it's very real. I'm particularly interested in visiting the museum."

"I think you'll find we have some very unusual exhibits," Armand put in.

"Yes, sir. I did some research before leaving England. I have no doubt that my time in Cordina will be an education."

Marissa toddled over, still a bit unsteady on her year-old legs, and held her arms up. Hannah placed the child in her lap.

"Your father is well?" Reeve asked her through a haze of smoke.

Hannah jangled her pearls to entertain the baby. "Yes, thank you. It often seems that the older I get, the younger he gets."

"Families, no matter how large or how small, are often the focus of our lives," Reeve said quietly.

"Yes, that's true," Hannah murmured as she played with the baby. "It's a pity that families, and life, aren't as simple as they seem when we're children."

Bennett sat relaxed in his chair and wondered why he thought if he could read between the lines, he'd discover a great deal more than small talk.

"I wasn't aware you knew Hannah's father, Reeve."

"Only casually." When he leaned back, his smile was easy. "I heard that Dorian stole your yo-yo again."

"I should have locked it in the safe when I heard he was coming." Bennett patted the slight bulge in his pocket. "I'd have given the little devil a run for his money, but he had an accomplice." He turned his head to look at Hannah.

"I'll have to apologize for my son," Gabriella's lips curved as she lifted her glass again. "For drawing you into his crime, Lady Hannah."

"On the contrary, I enjoyed it. Prince Dorian is charming."

"We call him other things at home," Reeve murmured. The woman was a mystery, he thought. The harder he looked for chinks, the fewer flaws he saw. "With that in mind, I think I'll go out and look for the bunch of them. Adrienne's at the age where you can't be sure she'll mind them or urge them to wade in the fountain."

Bennett glanced toward the terrace doors. "God knows what havoc they might have wrought in the last twenty minutes."

"Wait until you have your own." Eve rose to take Marissa from Hannah. "You'll spoil them rotten. If you'll excuse me, I want to go up and feed Marissa."

"I'll go with you." Gabriella set her glass aside. "I thought we might talk over the plans for the Christmas Ball. You know I want to help as much as I can."

"Thank God I don't have to beg. No, Hannah, please, sit and relax," Eve continued as Hannah started to stand. "We won't be long."

"See that you're not." Bennett took out the yo-yo to pass it from hand to hand. "Dinner's in an hour."

"We all know your priorities, Ben." Eve bent to kiss his cheek before she left the room.

"I could use a walk myself." Rising, Alexander nodded to Reeve. "I'll help you round up the children." They were barely out the terrace doors when a servant appeared in the doorway.

"I beg your pardon, Your Highness. A call from Paris."

"Yes, I've been expecting it. I'll take it in my office, Louis. If you'll excuse me, Lady Hannah." Taking her hand, Armand bowed over it. "I'm sure Bennett can entertain you for a few moments. Bennett, perhaps Lady Hannah would enjoy seeing the library."

"If you like to look at walls of books," Bennett said when his father was gone, "you can't do much better."

"I'm very fond of books." Taking him at his word, Hannah rose.

"All right then." Though he could have thought of a dozen better ways to while away an hour, he took her arm and led her through the corridors.

"It's difficult to believe that the museum could have finer paintings than you have here in the palace, Prince Bennett."

"Le Musée D'Art has a hundred and fifty-two examples of Impressionist and Postimpressionist paintings, including two Corots, three Monets and a particularly fine Renoir. We've recently acquired a Childe Hassam from the United States. In return my family has donated six Georges Complainiers, a Cordinian artist who painted on the island in the nineteenth century."

"I see."

Noting her expression, Bennett laughed. "As it happens, I'm on the board of the museum. I may prefer horses, Hannah, but that doesn't preclude an affection for art. What do you think of this?"

He paused in front of a small watercolor. The Royal Palace was beautifully, almost mystically painted. Its white, white walls and turrets rose behind a pink mist that enchanted rather than concealed the building itself. It must have been dawn, she thought. The sky was such a delicate blue in contrast to the deeper sea. She could see the antiquity, the fantasy and the reality. In the foreground were the high iron gates and sturdy stone walls that protected the palace grounds.

"It's beautiful. It shows love as well as a touch of wonder. Who was the artist?"

"My great-great-grandmother." Pleased with her reaction, Bennett drew her hand into the crook of his arm. "She'd done hundreds of watercolors and had tucked them away. In her day, women painted or drew as a hobby, not as a profession."

"Some things change," Hannah murmured, then looked back at the painting. "Some things don't."

"A few years ago I found her work in a trunk in one of the attics. So many of them had been damaged. It broke my heart. Then I found this." He touched the frame, reverently, Hannah thought. She looked from his hand to his face and found herself caught up in him. "It was like stepping back in time, generations, and discovering yourself. It could have been painted today, and it would look the same."

She could feel her heart moving toward him. What woman was immune to pride and sensitivity? In defense, she took a small step back. "In Europe, we understand that a few generations are only a blink in time. Our history stands before us, centuries of it. It becomes our responsibility to give that same gift to each new generation."

Bennett looked at her and found her eyes almost impossibly deep. "We do have that in common, don't we? In America, there's an urgency that can be exciting, even contagious, but here, we know how long it takes to build and secure. Politics change, governments shift, but history stands firm."

She had to turn away from him. It would only cloud the issue if she thought of him as a caring, sensitive man rather than an assignment. "Are there any others?" she said with a nod toward the painting.

"Only a handful, unfortunately. Most were beyond repair." For reasons he could only be half-sure of, he wanted to share with her things that mattered to him. "There's one in the music room. The rest are in the museum. Here, have a look." With his hand guiding her again, he took her down the hall into the next wing, their footsteps echoing off the mosaic tile.

Leading her through an open door, Bennett took her into a room that seemed to have been fashioned to accent the white grand piano in its center.

There was a harp in the corner that might have been played a hundred years before, or last week. In a glass case were antique wind instruments and a fragile lyre. The flowers were fresh here, as they were in every room in the palace. Trailing blossoms of jasmine spilled out of glossy, Chinese red urns. A small marble fireplace was swept and scrubbed clean with a pile of fresh kindling stacked as though inviting the match.

With Bennett, she walked across an Aubusson carpet to look back in time. This painting was of a ball, festive in bright colors and bold strokes. Women, gloriously feminine in mid-nineteenth-century gowns, were whirled around a gleaming floor by dashing men. There were mirrors that reflected the dancers and doubled them while a trio of chandeliers glistened overhead. As Hannah studied it, she could almost hear the waltz.

"How lovely. Is this room here, in the palace?"

"Yes. It has hardly changed. We'll have the Christmas Ball there next month."

Only a month, she thought. There was so much to be done. In a matter of hours Deboque would be out of prison, and she would soon learn if her groundwork had been clever enough.

"This is a beautiful room." Hannah turned. Keep your conversation light, she warned herself. Keep your mind light, for now. "In our country house there's a small music room. Nothing like this, of course, but I've always found it so relaxing." She wandered to the piano, not so much to examine it as to give herself distance. "Do you play, Your Highness?"

"Hannah, we're alone. It isn't necessary to be so formal."

"I've always considered the use of titles as proper rather than formal." She didn't want this, she thought quickly. She didn't want him to close that gap of rank between them.

"I've always considered it annoying between friends." He walked behind her to touch her lightly on the shoulder. "I thought we were."

She could feel his hand right through the neat linen of her dress, through the skinny silk strap beneath and onto her flesh. Fighting her own private war, she kept her back to him. "Were what, sir?"

He laughed, then both hands were on her shoulders, turning her to face him. "Friends, Hannah. I find you good company. That's one of the first requirements of friendship, isn't it?"

She was looking up at him, solemn-eyed, with the faintest blush of color along her cheekbones. Her shoulders seemed so strong under his hands, yet he remembered how soft, how delicate the skin along her jawline had seemed.

Her dress was brown and dull, her face unpainted and unframed. Not a hair was out of place and yet he got a flash of her laughing, her hair unbound and her shoulders bare. And the laughter would be for only him.

"What the devil is it about you?" Bennett muttered.

"I beg your pardon—"

"Wait." Impatient, as annoyed with himself as he was with her, Bennett stepped closer. As she stiffened, he held his hands up, palms out as if to reassure her he meant her no harm. "Just be still a moment, would you?" he asked as he lowered his head and touched his mouth to hers.

No response, show no response. Hannah repeated it over and over in her head like a litany. He didn't press, he didn't coax or demand. He simply tasted, more gently than she'd had known a man could be. And the flavor of him seeped into her until she was all but drunk with it.

His eyes remained open, watching hers. He was close, so close she could catch the scent of soap on his skin. Something that brought images of the sea. Hannah dug her fingers into her palms and fought to keep from showing him the turmoil within.

God, she wanted. How she wanted.

He didn't know what he'd expected. What he found was softness, comfort, sweetness without heat or passion. Yet he saw both in her eyes. He felt no driving need to touch her or to deepen the kiss. Not this first one. Perhaps he already knew there would be others. But this first one showed him an ease, a relaxation that he'd never looked for in a woman before.

He was man enough, experienced enough, to know there was a volcano inside of her. But strangely, he had no desire to push it to the eruption point, yet.

Bennett broke the kiss simply by stepping back. Hannah didn't move a muscle.

"I didn't do that to frighten you." He spoke quietly, for it was the truth. "It was just a test."

"You don't frighten me." He didn't frighten the woman he could see, but the one within was terrified.

It wasn't quite the answer he'd wanted. "Then what do I do to you?"

Slowly, carefully, she unballed her hands. "I'm afraid I don't understand what you mean, Your Highness."

He studied her another moment, then spun away. "Maybe not." He rubbed a hand along the back of his neck wondering why such an unassuming, placid woman should make him so tense. He understood desire. God knows he'd felt it before. But not like this. Never quite like this.

"Dammit, Hannah, isn't anything going on inside of you?"

"Of course, sir, a great number of things."

He had to laugh. He should have known she would put him in his place with logic. "Call me by my name, please."

"As you wish."

He turned back. She was standing in front of the glistening white piano, hands folded, eyes calm and quiet on his. He thought it the most ridiculous thing, but knew he was very close to falling in love. "Hannah—"

He'd taken no more than two steps toward her when Reeve walked into the room. "Bennett, excuse me, but your father would like to see you before dinner."

Duty and desire. Bennett wondered if he would ever find a full merging of the two. "Thank you, Reeve."

"I'll take Lady Hannah back in."

"All right." Still, he paused and looked at her again. "I'd like to talk with you later."

"Of course." She would move heaven and earth to avoid it.

She remained where she was when he left. Reeve glanced over his shoulder before he came closer. "Is there a problem, Lady Hannah?"

"No." She drew a deep breath, but didn't relax. "Why should there be?"

"Bennett can be . . . distracting."

This time when her eyes met his, she made certain they were slightly amused. A layer, the thinnest of the layers of her outer covering was dismissed. "I'm not easily distracted, particularly when I'm working."

"So I've been told," Reeve said easily enough. He was still looking for flaws and was afraid he might have found the first in the way she had looked at Bennett. "But you've never worked on an assignment quite like this one."

"As a senior agent for the ISS, I'm capable of handling any assignment." Her voice was brisk again, not the voice of a woman who'd been moved, almost unbearably, by a kiss. "You'll have my report by tomorrow. Now I think we'd better join the others."

She started by, but he took her arm and stopped her. "There's a great deal riding on this. On you."

Hannah only nodded. "I'm aware of that. You requested the best, and I am."

"Maybe." But the closer it came, the more he worried. "You've got a hell of a reputation, Hannah, but you've never come up against anyone like Deboque before."

"Nor he anyone like me." She glanced toward the hallway again, then lowered her voice. "I'm an established member of his organization now. It's taken me two years to get this close. I saved him two and a half million by seeing that that munitions deal wasn't botched six months ago. A man like Deboque appreciates initiative. In the last few months, I've been planting the seeds that will discredit his second in command."

"Or get your throat cut."

"That's for me to worry about. In a matter of weeks, I'll be his right hand. Then I'll serve him to you on a platter."

"Confidence is an excellent weapon, if it isn't overdone."

"I don't overdo." She thought of Bennett and strengthened her resolve. "I've never failed with an assignment, Reeve. I don't intend to begin with this one."

"Just make sure you keep in contact. I'm sure you'll understand when I say I don't trust anyone."

"I understand perfectly, because neither do I. Shall we go?"

Chapter Four

Hannah's plans to avoid driving with Bennett to Le Havre were neatly demolished. She'd justified her decision by convincing herself she could detail more useful information by concentrating on the palace. In order to remain behind, she'd come up with the credible, if unoriginal excuse of a headache.

Hannah had deliberately waited until Alexander had finished breakfasting with his family so that she could speak to Eve alone. It took Eve less than ten minutes to turn it on her.

"It's no wonder you're not feeling yourself." Eve sipped tea in the sunny nursery while she looked over her schedule. "I've kept you cooped up ever since you arrived."

"Don't be silly. The palace is the size of a small town. I've hardly been cooped up."

"However big it is, it still has walls. A nice drive along the coast is just what you need. Bernadette." She glanced up at the young nurse who was preparing to take Marissa for her morning walk. "Would you see that Princess Marissa has a hat? It's a bit breezy out."

"Yes, ma'am."

Eve held out her arms for her daughter. "Have a nice time, darling."

"Flowers," Marissa said, and laughed at her own voice.

"Yes, pick some flowers. We'll put them right here in your room." She kissed both of Marissa's cheeks then let her go. "I hate not being able to take her for a walk this morning, but I have a meeting at the Center in an hour."

"You're a wonderful mother, Eve," Hannah murmured when she saw the concern in Eve's eyes.

"I love her so much." With a long sigh, she picked up her tea again. "I know it's foolish, but when I'm not with her I think of dozens of things that might happen, that could happen."

"I'd say it was normal."

"Maybe. Being who we are, what we are, just magnifies everything." Unconsciously, she rested her hand where even now her second child slept. "I want so badly to give her a sense of normalcy, and yet..." Eve shook her head. "There's a price for everything."

Hannah remembered Alexander saying almost the same thing in referring to his wife.

"Eve, Marissa is a lovely, healthy and happy child. I'm not sure they get any more normal than that."

Eve stared at her a moment, then dropped her chin on her open palm. "Oh, Hannah, I'm not sure how I got through the last two years without you. Which brings me right back to where we were." Briskly, Eve refilled Hannah's cup. "You came here to visit and so far I haven't given you a moment's free time unless you were handcuffed to me. That makes me feel very selfish."

"The reason I'm here is to be with you," Hannah reminded Eve, as she felt herself rapidly losing ground.

"The reason you're here is because we're friends. As a favor, take the day, relax, enjoy the sea air. I promise you Ben can be wonderful company. I guarantee that five minutes after you're in the car, your headache will disappear."

"Someone have a headache?" Ben asked as he strode in. He was wearing the white dress uniform with the red insignia that stated his rank as officer in the Cordinian Navy. On the left breast pocket was the royal seal that proclaimed him prince. Hannah had always considered the opinion that women fell for men in uniform nonsense. Until now.

He looked so... dashing, she admitted, though her practical side searched for a less dramatic word. The snowy-white jacket accented his tan and the dark contrast of his hair. He grinned at her, making Hannah aware that he understood his effect. Automatically she rose to dip into a curtsy.

"Bennett, I'd forgotten what a heartbreaker you are in dress whites." Eve tipped her face up for a kiss. "Maybe I should tell Hannah to take an aspirin and stay behind after all."

"I think Lady Hannah can take care of herself. Can't you, *chérie*?"

Hannah decided then and there that if she had to fence with him, she would wield her foil well. "It's always been the case."

"You are a bit pale." He touched a finger to her cheek. "Are you really not well?"

"It's nothing." She wondered if he could feel her blood stir at the casual contact. "And Eve assures me that a drive along the sea is exactly the right prescription."

"Good. I'll bring her back with roses in her cheeks."

"If you'll give me a moment, I need to get my bag."

"Bennett." Eve stopped him before he could follow Hannah out. "Am I wrong, or did I see something just now?"

He didn't pretend to misunderstand her. "I'm not sure."

"Hannah's lived a very sheltered life. I suppose I don't have to tell you to be... well, careful?"

Though the sunlight streamed in behind him, his eyes cooled. "No, I don't have to be reminded who a man in my position can and can't have an affair with."

"I didn't say that to annoy you." Instantly Eve was on her feet, taking his hands. "We were friends long before we were family, Ben. I only ask because I'm fond of her and I know how irresistible you can be."

He softened, as he always did with Eve. "You always managed to resist."

"You always treated me like a sister." Eve hesitated again, torn between two loyalties. "Would I be pushing if I said she's not your usual type?"

"No, she's not. Perhaps that's what baffles me. Stop worrying." He bent to kiss her brow. "I won't damage your proper British friend."

"It could be I'm just as concerned about you."

"Then don't be." Giving her cheek a careless stroke, he walked to the door. "Tell Marissa I'll bring her some seashells."

Calm and resigned to her decision, Hannah met him at the top of the stairs. "I hope I didn't keep you waiting."

"We've plenty of time. I can promise the drive will be worth the pomp and speeches on the other end."

"I don't object to pomp and speeches."

"Then we're fortunate. Claude." Bennett nodded to the tall, sturdy man who waited beside the main doors.

"Good morning, Your Highness. Lady Hannah. Your car is ready, sir."

"Thank you, Claude." Bennett steered Hannah through the doors knowing the simple statement meant that the road between Cordina and Le Havre had been secured.

Hannah saw the car the moment they stepped outside. The zippy little French convertible sat at the foot of the steps flanked by two solid sedans.

"Do you drive that?"

"Looks like I should wind it up, doesn't it?" Bennett touched the shiny red hood with affection. "Handles like a dream. I've had her up to one-twenty on a straight."

She thought of how it would feel, speeding beside the sea with the wind on her face. Hannah pushed aside such wishes and tried for an uneasy look. "I hope you don't intend to try to break your record today."

With a laugh, he opened the door for her himself. "For you, I'll drive like a grandfather."

Hannah slipped into the seat and nearly sighed with pleasure. "It is rather small."

"Big enough for two." Bennett rounded the hood. Claude already had his door opened.

"But surely you don't travel without your security or an assistant."

"Whenever possible. My secretary will be in the car behind us. Let's give them a run, shall we?" He switched on the ignition. From the rich sound under the hood, Hannah decided it was filled with engine. Before she could draw a breath, Bennett sent the car speeding down the long, sedate drive. He drove the way he rode a stallion. Full speed.

"They're muttering already, I imagine." He gave the guards at the gates an easy salute. "If Claude had his way, I'd never go over thirty kilometers. I'd also be closed up in a bulletproof limo wearing a suit of armor."

"It's his job to protect you."

"A pity he has so little humor about it." Bennett downshifted, then sent the car squeaking around a curve.

"Did your grandfather live a long and fruitful life?"

"What?"

"Your grandfather," Hannah repeated as she folded her hands neatly in her lap. "I wondered if he lived a long life. It seems unlikely if he drove like this."

The wind was blowing his hair around his face as he turned his head to grin at her. "Trust me, *ma belle*, I know the roads."

She didn't want him to slow down. It was the first time she'd felt true freedom in months. She'd nearly forgotten how sweet it tasted. The sea shimmered blue and white beside the road as they traveled down from the heights of the capital. Palms twisted their way toward the sky, bending and swaying in the stiff breeze. Lush red flowers burst out of bushes that grew helter-skelter along the roadside. The air smelled of sea and perpetual spring.

"Do you ski?" Bennett asked her as he noticed her watching a man glide over the water behind a low-slung boat.

"I never have." It looked wonderful. "I'm sure you have to be fairly athletic. I'm more at home in libraries."

"One can't read all the time."

She watched the skier take a somersaulting tumble into the water. "I think perhaps I can."

Bennett grinned and roared though a lazy S-turn. "Life's hardly worth the trouble without a few spills. Don't you ever have the urge for adventure, Hannah?"

She thought of the last ten years of her life, of the assignments that had taken her from castles to ghettos and everywhere in between. French alleys. Italian waterfronts. She thought of the small-caliber pistol she carried in her bag and the pencil-slim stiletto tucked like a lover against her thigh.

"I suppose I've always preferred my adventures vicariously, through books."

"No secret dreams?"

"Some of us are exactly what we seem." Suddenly uncomfortable, she shifted away from the topic. "I didn't realize you were a naval officer." Another lie, she thought. But her profession was built on them.

"I served a couple of years. At this point, it's more of an honorary rank. Second sons are traditionally bound for the military."

"So you chose the navy."

"Cordina's surrounded by the sea. Our fleet is smaller than yours, certainly, but it's strong."

"And these are uneasy times."

Something came and went in his eyes. "In Cordina we've learned that all times are uneasy times. We're a peaceful country, and because we want to remain so, we're prepared always for war."

She thought of the pretty white palace with its exotic gardens and fairy-tale turrets. Inaccessible by sea, with a cliff-top view that scanned miles with the naked eye. She sat back as the sea rolled by. Nothing ever was as simple as it seemed.

Le Havre was charming. Nestled at the base of a long hill, it clustered together with small white-washed buildings and clapboard cottages. Fishing and sail boats swayed quietly at neat docks at one curve of the harbor. Around the seawall of old stone, hardy blue flowers pushed their way through cracks. There were lobster traps and nets spread and drying in the sun. The scent of fish was heady and oddly pleasant in the early morning air.

At a glance, it could have been taken for any tidy fishing town that survived on and with the sea. But as they rounded the harbor the docks became more expansive, the buildings larger. Cargo ships with men hauling freight down gangplanks flanked an ocean liner. Like much of Cordina, Le Havre was more than it seemed. Through location and the skill of its people, it was one of the finest ports of call in the Mediterranean. It was also the center of Cordina's naval base.

Negotiating the narrow, winding streets, Bennett drove through a set of gates. He slowed only long enough to be acknowledged by the guards with snappy salutes. There were bungalows here painted a faded pink that reminded Hannah of the inside of a seashell. Palms and flowers grew in profusion, but she recognized the structure and order of a military facility. Moments later, Bennett drew up in front of a stucco building where seamen in whites stood at attention.

"For the next few hours," he murmured to Hannah, "we're official." Bennett reached in the back and picked up his hat. Even as he set it on his wind-ruffled hair, one of the

seamen reached the door to open it for him. With the brim
shading his eyes, Bennett returned the salutes. He knew the
sedan had already pulled up behind him, but didn't look
back as he guided Hannah into the building.

"First, we have a few formalities," he warned her, tuck-
ing his hat under his arm.

The formalities were a group of officers, from admiral
down, and their wives and attachés who were waiting to
greet and be greeted by His Royal Highness.

Hannah acknowledged the introductions and pretended
not to see the looks of speculation. *Not the prince's type.*
She could read it easily in every eye that met hers. She fully
agreed.

They were given tea and a tour of the building—for her
sake. Hannah feigned an ignorance of the equipment shown
her, asking the proper questions and looking properly polite at the simplistic answers. She could hardly mention that
the radar and communication systems were as familiar to
her as they were to the trained operators. In a pinch, she
could have rigged the equipment to contact the ISS base
outside London or Deboque's headquarters in Athens.

She walked by display cases, listening with apparent fascination as an admiral explained to her the difference between a destroyer and an aircraft carrier.

The pomp and circumstance continued as they were escorted outside to await the docking of the *Indépendance.*
The band, their white uniforms blinding in the sun, struck
up a rousing march as Bennett stepped onto the dock.
Crowds of people cheered from behind the military barri-
cade. Babies and small children were held up so that they
could catch a glimpse of the prince.

Hannah counted off a dozen security people mingled with
the crowd in addition to the two men who were never more
than an arm's span from Bennett's elbow.

Deboque is out, she thought. Everything is a risk.

The battle-gray destroyer maneuvered into position while the crowd applauded and the band continued to play. Seamen on the dock stood at attention as did seamen on deck. After six months at sea, the *Indépendance* was home.

The gangplank came ponderously down. The pipes were sounded. The captain strode down to salute the officers and bow to his prince.

"Welcome home, Captain." Bennett offered his hand, and the crowd cheered again.

There was, as there always was on such occasions, a speech to be made. Hannah kept her face attentive while she slowly scanned the crowd.

It was no surprise to find him there. The small, slightly stoop-shouldered man was on the edge of the crowd holding a small Cordinian flag. In his plain work clothes and quiet face, he would never be noticed or remembered. He was one of Deboque's best.

There would be no move on Prince Bennett today, she thought, though the back of her neck itched. Her successful planting at the palace had been one of her highest contributions to Deboque's organization. The working order now was for care and cleverness rather than a rash assassination attempt.

In any case, she knew Deboque wasn't as interested in Bennett as he was in Alexander, and in Alexander not so much as in Armand. He wouldn't settle for the second in line to the throne after so long a wait.

Still, she closed her hand over the handle of her bag. She shifted, only a matter of inches, but Bennett's body was now more than half shielded by hers.

Had the man been sent with a message for her? Hannah wondered. Or had he simply been ordered to stay close and watch? Instinct told her it was the second. Casually, she swept the crowd again. Her eyes met his and held for only a fraction of a second. There was an acknowledgement, but no signal. Hannah let her gaze move on, knowing they'd meet within a few days at the museum.

The pretty ceremony with its brisk military music and banners continued with a tour of the ship and an inspection of the crew. Hannah walked with the admiral's wife as Bennett was led down the line of officers and seamen. Now and then he stopped to comment or ask a personal question of one of the men. More, she saw that he listened to the answers. Even a casual observer could have seen that he was given more than respect due his rank by the men he greeted. There was love, the kind Hannah was aware only men could give men.

Though she was certain Bennett had seen enough of ships to last a lifetime, he toured the bridge, the officers' quarters and the galleys with apparent fascination. The ship was as neat as a parlor, utilitarian certainly, but freshly scrubbed and without a sign of peeling paint or rust.

Bennett moved quickly through the ship, without seeming to hurry over the decks. There were questions that had to be asked, compliments that were deserved, but he knew duffle bags were packed and waiting. He clasped hands with the captain again, aware that the man had every right to be proud of his ship and his men. As he started down the gangplank, the cheers rose up again. Bennett had to wonder if they were for him or because the ceremonies were finally over and the men could go ashore.

Protocol demanded that he be escorted back through headquarters. It was here that Hannah began to sense his impatience to be off. Still, he was gracious, shaking hands, kissing hands, exchanging a last pleasantry. It wasn't until he was seated in his own car again that he let out a low oath.

"I beg your pardon, sir?"

Bennett merely patted Hannah's hand before he started the engine. "Four hours was a long time to keep you on your feet. Thank you for bearing with me."

"On the contrary, I found it fascinating." Nothing had ever seemed more wonderful than the wind blowing on her face again as the convertible picked up speed. "The tour of the ship was particularly educational. It was clever, wasn't it, for the ship's cook to frame a recipe for crepes where the flour was measured in pounds rather than cups?"

"Food becomes a priority after a few months at sea." He glanced over, surprised she'd been so well entertained by a ship and several pompous speeches. "If I'd known you were really interested I wouldn't have hurried things along quite so much."

"I suppose it becomes all routine and a bit boring for you after a while."

"I was thinking of the men. All they really wanted was to get ashore to their wives or lovers—or both." He was grinning when he turned his head toward her. "You can't imagine what four months at sea is like when the only woman you see is in a glossy photo with staple marks in the middle."

Her lips twitched, but she managed to hold the smile to a bare acknowledgement. "No, I'm sure I can't. But I think you enjoyed your time at sea, Bennett. It showed in the way you spoke with the men and looked at the ship."

He said nothing for a moment, surprised and not displeased that she had understood that so quickly. "I was more of an officer and less of a prince then. I can't say I have the sea in my blood the way Captain Dumont does, but it isn't something I'll forget."

"What is it you remember best?" she asked before she caught herself.

"Watching the sun rise at sea or better, riding out a storm. God, we went through one off Crete. The waves were a fifty-foot wall. The wind was like the wrath of God, so loud, so enormous that you could shout in someone's ear and not be heard. No sky, only water, wall after wall of it. An experience like that changes you."

"How?"

"It makes you realize that no matter who you are, what you are, there's something bigger, greater. Nature's a powerful equalizer, Hannah. Look at her now." With one hand he gestured toward the sea as he negotiated another curve. "Calm, almost impossibly beautiful. A hurricane doesn't make her less beautiful, only more dangerous."

"It sounds as though you prefer the danger." She understood that, perhaps too well.

"At times. Danger's its own seduction."

She could say nothing to that. It was something she had learned herself years before.

With the briefest of signals to the car behind him, Bennett pulled over. "At the moment I prefer the calm." He got out of the convertible, ignoring the guard who stood anxiously by the hood of the trailing car. "Walk with me on the beach, Hannah." He opened her door and held out a hand. "I promised Marissa some shells."

"Your security doesn't look pleased." Nor was she when she noticed how open they were.

"They'd only be pleased if I were sitting in a bulletproof globe. Come now, Hannah, didn't you tell me sea air was good for the constitution?"

"Yes." She laid her hand in his. He was safe, after all, as long as she played her part and played it well. "You'll have to find shells big enough that they can't be swallowed. At Marissa's age, children tend to eat the oddest things."

"Always practical." With an easy laugh, he lifted her by the waist over the low seawall. He saw her gaze focus over his shoulder and knew a guard would be following at a discreet distance. "You should take your shoes off, Hannah. You'll only get sand in them."

It was the practical thing to do, of course. The logical thing. Hannah tried to tell herself she wasn't shedding part of her cover along with the pumps. "You must have some fascinating coral formations in these waters."

"Do you scuba?"

"No," she lied. "I'm not a very strong swimmer. I went to a marine exhibit in London a few years ago. Until then, I had no idea what an incredible variety of shells there were, or how valuable they can be."

"Lucky for me Marissa has simple tastes." With his hand on hers, he walked to the sea edge. "A couple of clam shells, and she'll be delighted."

"It's kind of you to think of her." He *was* kind, she thought. That itself was one of the most difficult things to overlook. "You seem to be a great favorite among your nieces and nephews."

"Oh, I suppose that's because I don't mind making a fool of myself now and then in a game. How about this one?" Bending, he picked up a long spiral that had broken off a larger shell and been worn smooth by the ebb and flow of the sea. At the top of the curve was a peaked cap that looked almost like a crown.

"Very suitable," Hannah commented when he handed it to her.

"Marissa doesn't care for suitable. She prefers pretty."

"It is pretty." With a smile, Hannah ran a finger along the curve that went from pale amber to polished pink. "She should have it in her windowsill where the sun would hit it. Oh look." Forgetting herself, she stepped into the surf and pried out an unbroken scallop shell. It was shaped like a fan, bone-white on one side, opalescent pink inside its shallow bowl. "You could tell her that fairies take their biscuits in it when they have tea."

"So Hannah believes in fairies," he murmured.

Caught up short, she handed him the shell. "No, but I think Marissa might."

Bennett slipped the shell into his pocket. "Your feet are wet."

"They'll dry quickly enough." She started to step back. He took her hand again, holding her in the shallow, foaming surf.

"Since we're here, we ought to try for a couple more." Without waiting for a response he began to walk along the shoreline.

The water was warm and soft on her feet and ankles, but no warmer, no softer, than the air that blew in over it. Through the crystal water she could see the bed of white sand and the glittering sparkles of shells that had been crushed by waves. The surf was quiet here, all sighs and whispers.

There was nothing romantic in it, Hannah warned herself. She couldn't allow there to be. The line she walked was thinner and sharper than any she'd walked before. One misstep could mean tragedy at least, war at the worst. Determined to keep her place, she concentrated on the guards a few yards at their back.

"The ceremony today was lovely. I'm grateful you asked me to come."

"My reasons were purely selfish. I wanted your company."

Struggling not to be touched, she tried again. "In England there's often satire and criticism of the Royal Family, but beneath it all is a very real affection. I see that same kind of love and respect for your family here."

"My father would tell you that we serve as well as govern. He gives them solidity and confidence. Alex gives them the hope for the future. A continuation of tradition. In Brie they have glamor and intelligence as well as humanity."

"And in you?"

"Entertainment."

It annoyed her. She couldn't say why but his careless dismissal of himself made her stop and frown at him. "You underestimate yourself."

Surprised, Bennett cocked his head and studied her. It was there again, that something, that indefinable something in her eyes that had attracted him all along. "Not really. I'm well aware that I do my duty. My father raised all of us to understand that we didn't simply inherit a title or position. We had to earn it." He drew her back a bit so that the spray from the surf didn't dampen her skirt. "I won't rule. Thank God. That's for Alex and then for the son I continue to hope Eve gives us all this time around. Because I won't, I don't have to take myself as seriously as Alex, but that doesn't mean I take Cordina or my responsibilities to it lightly."

"I didn't mean to criticize."

"I didn't think you did. I only meant that above my official duties, my official position, I give the people something—someone to talk about over a glass of wine or an evening meal. I've been haunted by the title of Playboy Prince since I was in my teens." He grinned then and tucked a stray hair behind her ear. "I can't say I didn't do everything possible to earn it."

"I prefer literature to gossip," Hannah said primly as she started to walk on.

"Gossip has its place." Amused, Bennett stopped her.

"Apparently you enjoy it."

"No." His eyes darkened as he looked beyond her and out to sea. "I'm just accustomed to it. It's difficult, when you're twenty, to know that every time you look more than casually at a woman it's going to be splashed somewhere in bold print, pictures included. I like women." This time he smiled and looked back at her. "Since I didn't want to change that aspect of my personality, I decided to live with public speculation. If I've sinned, it was in lack of discretion."

"Some might say it was the quantity."

There was only the shortest of hesitations before he threw his head back and roared with laughter. "Oh, Hannah, what a gem you are. So you *have* whiled away some time with something besides Yeats."

"I may have skimmed a few headlines."

Laughing again, he swung her in a circle before she could prevent it. "Priceless. Absolutely priceless." His eyes were glowing as he set her back down. "I adore how you cut me down to size so skillfully."

Automatically, Hannah smoothed down her skirt. "I'm sure you've mistaken my intent."

"The devil I have. That's what delights me about you."

The frustrated look she gave him had nothing to do with the role she was playing. Delighting him had never been part of the plan. She was there to observe, to cement her position and to carry out a plan that was years in the making. Never before had the proper Lady Hannah had to worry about piquing a man's interest. Even as she calculated how to cancel it out again, he was reaching for her.

"Your hair's falling down." In a casual move he plucked a loose pin that was dangling near her shoulder. "My fault for not putting the top up."

"I must look as though I've been through a hurricane." She reached up to put the practical hairstyle back in place. Pins fell out in her hand, loosened by wind and weight. Even as she swore silently, her hair tumbled free, waterfalling past her shoulders to her waist.

"*Mon Dieu.*" Before she could twist her hair back, Bennett had filled both hands with it. Twined around his fingers it was deep, honey blond and soft as silk. He stared, thunderstruck, by the transformation. It waved wild and free around her face, accenting the slash of cheekbones that only looked hard and angular without the framing. Her face no longer seemed thin and bony, but exotic. *"C'est magnifique. C'est la chevelure d'un ange."*

With her heart pounding, she tried to ignore what she saw in his eyes. It wasn't innocent delight or casual attraction now. Now there was desire, man for woman, basic, strong and as dangerous as the sea in a storm. She couldn't move back from him for his hands were buried in her hair. She couldn't deny the lunge of her own needs as he kept her close.

It wasn't supposed to happen. Even now she could tell herself it couldn't happen. Yet she wanted to be held by him, to be comforted, to be, though the words sounded foolish in her mind, cherished. Desired, needed, loved. All of those things were against the rules, but she found it hard to pull back.

"Angel hair," Bennett repeated in a whisper. "Why does a woman bind beauty up and hide it?"

No, she couldn't deny what was happening inside her, but she could, as she'd been trained, deny herself. "It's more practical worn up." She lifted her hands to scoop it from his and met resistance.

Yes, he'd been right all along. There was more, much more to her than she allowed to show on the surface. Perhaps it was that which continued to draw him in, make him want, make him need in a way he never had before. If it had been possible, he would have pulled her to him then. It wasn't the guards that stopped him, but the trace of anxiety he saw in her eyes.

"If that was true, my most practical Hannah, why haven't you simply cut it off?"

How many times had she nearly done so then pulled back at the last minute? Drawing a deep breath she offered the simple truth because truth was often the best cover of all. "Even I have some vanity."

"It makes you beautiful." He dragged his hands through her hair again, hardly able to believe it had been hidden by a handful of pins.

"Only different." Her smile hid the tension that was pulling her in two directions.

"Any man would approve of such a difference." She was stiff beneath his hands. With reluctance he acknowledged it and released her. "But then, you don't look for a man's approval, do you?"

"I've never found it necessary." With a few expert twists, she had her hair at the base of her neck again. The pins were pushed in until it was secure. She could almost, just almost feel secure herself. "We should be getting back. Eve may need me."

With a nod, Bennett began to walk back to the car with her. There would be another time and another place. He found in himself something he experienced rarely, particularly when it had to do with a woman. Patience.

"You can pin it up, Hannah. But now that I know what it looks like down, I'll see it that way whenever I look at you." When they reached the seawall, he again lifted her over, but this time stood, his hands around her waist and the wall between them. "Knowing this one secret makes me wonder how many others you have, and how soon I'll find them."

Anxiety and desire were a powerful combination. She felt her heart thud with both. "I'm afraid you'll be disappointed, Bennett. I have no interesting secrets."

"We'll see," he said, before he vaulted easily over the seawall.

Chapter Five

It wasn't often Hannah yearned to be beautiful. Her work had given her a fine appreciation for the beauty of being unremarkable, even forgettable. Over the years, she'd experienced a twinge now and then, but only a twinge when she thought of soft colors and filmy dresses. It had always been possible to release the urge when she was off duty and out of the country. Then her appearance could be changed with a more discerning choice of color and cut and a few clever strokes with a makeup brush.

There could be no release now, and no yearning.

Hannah knew everyone would look wonderful for Eve's dinner party. An affair at the palace was meant to be elegant, even extravagant. Hannah had no doubt every woman who attended would strive to live up to the occasion. Every woman, of course, except her.

She'd already seen Eve's glittery black dress with its swirls of material from waist to ankle and its daring draping back. Gabriella would no doubt wear something delicate that would accent her fragile, feminine looks.

Then there was Chantel O'Hurley. Hannah was certain the actress would be stunning whether she chose silk or sackcloth. Remembering how Bennett had looked at her as he'd started down the stairs in the Center took no effort at all.

It shouldn't have mattered.

It mattered too much.

Lecturing herself, Hannah chose the best of the worst in a pale lavender gown with a fussy bodice that played down her curves. With her hair unpinned, it gave her the look of a wanton puritan. An image, she knew, that wouldn't go unnoticed. With only the smallest of sighs, she drew her hair back to begin the laborious job of braiding it into submission.

When it was neatly coiled at her neck, Hannah was satisfied that all traces of sexuality were tamed. She looked presentable, perfectly proper and sexless.

There could be no regrets, Hannah told herself as she slipped her pistol into her evening bag. Duty came above personal desire, and certainly far ahead of vanity.

He'd been waiting for her. The guests were being entertained in the Salle des Miroirs where they were served aperitifs by short-coated waiters. Both the cast and the crew of Eve's production had been invited so that conversation was a babble of noise underlaid with excitement.

Though impatient and distracted, Bennett performed his duty without a ripple. There were always polite questions to be asked, a hand to kiss and a joke to laugh at. Under usual circumstances, the party would have amused and entertained him, but...

Where was she? He found himself straining against the evening clothes he usually wore without a thought. All around him women glittered. Their scents mingled and mixed into one exotic fragrance that did nothing to tempt him. He wanted a moment alone with Hannah. He hadn't the least idea why it was so important, but he wanted it desperately.

He kept one eye on the doorway while he spoke with the wardrobe mistress. His gaze paused briefly on the ormolu clock while he listened to the director expound on the potential of Eve's play.

"Looking for me?" The sultry voice sounded in his ear just ahead of a cloud of scent.

"Chantel." Bennett kissed both her cheeks before drawing her back for a survey. "Stunning, as always."

"I do what I'm best at." Smiling, she accepted a glass from a passing waiter. Shimmering white left her shoulders bare, then dipped low enough to be tantalizing before it closely followed the subtle, feminine curves. "Your home is everything it's rumored to be." She lifted the wine to her lips as her gaze passed over the dozens of antique mirrors that graced the walls. "And how clever of you to choose such a room to entertain a group of narcissistic actors."

"We have our moments." He looked beyond her for a moment, but still saw no sign of Hannah. "I saw your last movie. You were extraordinary."

A woman who was accustomed to absorbing all of a man's attention knew instinctively when she had only a part of it. Still, Chantel only smiled and speculated. "I'm still waiting for you to come back to Hollywood."

"You seem to be keeping busy in the meantime." He reached in his pocket for a box of matches to light her cigarette. "How do you manage to divide your time among tennis stars, oilmen and producers?"

Chantel tilted her head as she blew out a thin stream of smoke. "Oh, much the same way I imagine you divide yours among countesses, marchesas and—was it a barmaid in Chelsea?"

Laughing, Bennett dropped the matches back in his pocket. "*Ma chère amie,* if either of us enjoyed all the incredible and innumerable affairs the press gifts us with, we'd be hospitalized."

With the true affection she felt for few men, Chantel touched a hand to his cheek. "To anyone else, I'd say speak for yourself. However, since we've never been lovers, regardless of the headlines to the contrary, I'll ask you how things are for you, romantically speaking."

"Confusing." At that moment, in the oval glass over Chantel's shoulder, he saw Hannah slip into the room. She looked like a dove lost in a group of peacocks. "Very confusing. Excuse me a moment, will you, love?"

"Of course." She'd seen which direction his attention had taken. "*Bonne chance,* Bennett."

A lifetime of experience allowed him to slip through the groups of people, exchanging a quick word, a smile or a murmured excuse without leaving any offense behind. Less than a minute after Hannah had settled into a corner, he was beside her.

"*Bonsoir,* Lady Hannah."

"Your Highness." She used his title and curtsied as protocol demanded. He caught her hands as she straightened, negating the formality.

"It's usual, when a woman is late, that she makes an entrance rather than slip into a corner."

Damn him for making her pulse skittish. Even as she tried to calm it again, she noted that more than one head was turned in their direction. So much for going unnoticed. "I prefer watching to being watched, sir."

"I prefer watching you." He signaled a waiter, then took a glass from the tray for her himself. "You move well, Hannah, as though you wouldn't make a sound in an empty room."

That had as much to do with her training in tae kwon do as her childhood lessons in ballet. "I was raised not to make disturbances." She accepted the glass because it freed one of her hands. "Thank you. This is a lovely room." She said it casually, as casual as the glance she sent sweeping over the guests. Her reflection was thrown back at her a dozen times. Hers, and Bennett's, close together.

"I've always been partial to it." Now that she was here, he was content. He'd almost heard the click of things falling into their proper place when he'd taken her hand in his. "As it happens it was another Bennett, some generations back, who started the collection. It seems he was miserably vain without much cause and continued to buy mirrors in hopes one would tell him a different story."

She had to laugh. For a moment she felt almost as though she belonged there with the gowns and the glass and the glamor. "I'd say you made that up, but it sounds foolish enough to be true."

"You have the most alluring laugh," he murmured. "It's a laugh that reminds me how you look with your hair down and your eyes dark."

She couldn't allow this. Hannah told herself she was foolish to be moved when she knew how clever he was with women. She was more foolish to be caught off guard when she knew what a dangerous game was being played. This time her voice was cool and formal.

"Shouldn't you see to your guests?"

"I have been." He passed his thumb gently over her knuckles. It was a small gesture and an intimate one that made her wish once again she could have been lovely for him. That she could, very simply, have been for him. "While I was waiting for you." He stepped closer. Because she was already wedged into a corner, there was no place to go. "You smell wonderful."

"Bennett, please." She almost lifted a hand to his chest before she remembered eyes were on them. In defense she lifted her glass instead.

"Hannah, I can't tell you how it pleases me to see you become unnerved. The only time you become at all unsure of yourself is when I'm just a bit too close."

It was true, and a bitter pill to swallow for a woman who survived by being sure of herself. "People are watching."

"Then walk in the gardens with me later, when we can be alone."

"I don't think that would be wise."

"Are you afraid I'd seduce you?"

There was both amusement and arrogance in his tone, but when Hannah looked back at him, she saw desire as well. She sipped again to moisten a throat that had gone bone-dry. "Not afraid. Uncomfortable seems a better word."

"It would give me great pleasure to make you uncomfortable, Hannah." His voice was low, a caress to accompany the brush of his lips over her knuckles. "I want to make love with you in some dark, quiet place. Very slowly and very gently."

The need sprinted inside of her until she had to fight off a shudder of anticipation. It could be like that, with him, it could be. If only...

There could be no "ifs" in her life. They meant uncertainty and uncertainty was lethal. Hannah, pulling herself steady by nerve ends, looked at him. He meant it. There was desire in his eyes—but more a kindness, a sweetness that was almost her undoing. She could marvel at the fact that he felt something real for her, that somehow, he'd looked beyond the surface and cared.

She could want it, but she couldn't accept it. There was only one way to stop what should never have started. She had to hurt him, and she had to do it now.

"I'm sure I should be flattered." Her voice was cool and calm again. "But if you'll forgive me, sir, I'm aware that your tastes are not very selective."

He stiffened his fingers on hers before he released her hand. She saw by his eyes that the arrow had hit its mark. "I'd appreciate an explanation for that, Hannah."

"The explanation seems obvious. Please let me pass, you'll cause a scene."

"I've caused one before." There was something new in his voice now. It was anger, certainly, but a reckless, heedless anger. Hannah knew that if she didn't play her game exactly right now, she'd find her name splashed in headlines for battling with Bennett in public.

"Very well." Setting her glass down on a nearby table, she folded her hands in her usual fashion. "I'm a woman, and therefore of some passing interest. To be blunt, the interest isn't returned."

"That's a lie."

"No." Firmer now, she cut him off. "Though it might be difficult for a man like you to understand, I'm a simple woman with simple values. As you told me yourself, your reputation precedes you." She paused just long enough to see him wince.

Oh, Bennett, I'm sorry. So sorry.

"I didn't come to Cordina to amuse you," she murmured as she took a step to the side.

He suddenly lifted his hand to stop her, and she waited. "You don't amuse me, Hannah."

"Then I must beg your pardon." Knowing it would be more insult than courtesy, she dipped into a curtsy. "If you'll excuse me now, sir, I'd like to speak with Eve."

He held her another moment. Hannah could feel his fury sear through his fingertips and burn her flesh. Then, in an instant, there was ice. "I won't keep you. Enjoy the evening."

"Thank you."

Despising herself, Hannah moved into the crowd. The lights were so brilliant, she told herself. That was why her eyes hurt.

"Lady Hannah, good evening." Reeve stepped beside her and took her arm. "Would you care for some wine?"

"Yes, thank you." Falling into step beside him, she accepted the glass he held out.

"Have you seen this collection of mirrors? I've always found these three particularly impressive. Are you all right?" he added in an undertone.

"Yes, they are lovely. I'm fine."

He cupped his hand around the end of a cigarette, glancing around casually to be certain no one was within earshot. "It looked as though you were having some trouble with Bennett."

"He's persistent." She sipped her wine, amazed that her nerves had yet to calm. "Surely this is eighteenth-century."

"Hannah." He pointed out another glass as they walked, but his voice softened. "I worked with your father when I first got my feet wet with the ISS. That makes me feel almost like family. Are you all right?"

"I will be." She drew a deep breath and smiled as if he'd said something amusing. "I caused him pain just now. I didn't enjoy it."

Reeve brushed a hand over hers in the most casual of gestures. The touch was as reassuring as a hug. "It's rare to get through an assignment without hurting someone."

"Yes, I know—the end justifies the means. Don't worry, I'll do my job."

"I wasn't worried."

"It would help a great deal if you'd see that Bennett was kept busy over the next week or so. Things should be coming to a head and I don't need him ..."

"Distracting you?"

"Interfering," Hannah corrected. She glanced in one of the mirrors and saw him across the room with Chantel. "Though I may very well have taken care of that myself. Excuse me."

He drove the horse hard, but still didn't find the level of release he'd been seeking. Swearing, Bennett plunged down the winding path, but neither joy nor excitement rode with him. Fury left little room.

He ached for her. He damned her to the devil and still ached for her. In the days that had passed since she'd turned him aside, the wanting hadn't eased. Now it was coated with self-derision and anger, but it hadn't eased.

He told himself she was a cold, insensitive prude with no generosity or heart. He saw her as she had been on the beach, with a shell in her hand, her eyes rich with laughter as the wind pulled pins from her hair.

He told himself she was hard as stone and just as unfeeling. Then he remembered how soft, how sweet her lips had been when his own had tasted them.

So he cursed her and rode harder.

The skies threatened rain, but he ignored them. It was the first time in days he'd been able to get away from obligations long enough to take Dracula out for more than cursory exercise. The wind whistled in off the sea and set waves dancing high.

He wanted the storm. By God, he wanted the wind and the rain and the thunder.

He wanted Hannah.

Imbécile! Only a fool wanted a woman when there was nothing returned. Only a madman thought of ways to have what had already been denied. He'd told himself all this before, but still he caught himself dreaming of ways he could gather her up and take her somewhere until he found the right way to show her.... Show her what? Bennett asked himself. Show her that it was different with her?

What woman would believe it?

Dozens, he thought, and his own laughter echoed bitterly behind him. He could certainly attest to that. But now when it was true, when it mattered the most, this woman wouldn't believe.

Because he'd acted like an idiot. Drawing the stallion to a halt, he stopped at a precipice over the sea and looked out. He'd pushed, too hard, too fast. It was humbling to admit he might have done so because he'd never met with a great deal of resistance before.

Women were drawn to him—because of the title and position. He wasn't so vain or so foolish not to know it. But they were also drawn to him because he enjoyed them. He liked their softness, their humor, their vulnerabilities. It was also true that he hadn't been intimate with as many as his reputation allowed, but there'd been enough women in his life for him to understand and appreciate that romance was a two-way street.

Hannah was young, inexperienced, sheltered. The term "Lady" wasn't merely a title, but a way of life. As far as men were concerned, it was doubtful she'd taken herself away from her books long enough to form any strong relationships.

With another oath, Bennett dragged a hand through his wind-tossed hair. And what had he done? He'd tried to seduce her at a dinner party. How could he have expected a woman of her breeding and sensitivity to be anything less than insulted? It had been the clumsiest, and perhaps the crudest of propositions.

Dracula danced impatiently, but Bennett held him steady another moment as he watched the storm roll slowly from the horizon toward the shore.

He hadn't told her, had never attempted to tell her what it was she did to him inside, to his heart. Just talking with her, watching that solemn face and quiet manner excited him in a way the most exotic or flamboyant woman never had. It was something deeper, and so much richer. He'd never said that with her, he was on the edge of finding the love he hadn't been sure would ever be there for him.

He could hardly do all of that now that he'd alienated and insulted her. But he could do something else. His smile began as the first drops of water hit the sea. He could start at the beginning.

Bennett wheeled the horse around. As the first streak of lightning split the sky, they were racing for home.

Within an hour, in dry clothes and dripping hair, Bennett made his way up to the nursery. Bernadette barred him at the door.

"Your pardon, Your Highness, but it's Princess Marissa's nap time. Her Highness is resting with the baby."

"I'm looking for Lady Hannah." He leaned into the room, but Bernadette stood her ground.

"Lady Hannah isn't here, sir. I believe she went to the museum this afternoon."

"The museum." Bennett calculated a moment. "Thank you, Bernadette."

Before she could finish her curtsy, he was gone.

Le Musée d'Art was small and lovely as was the rest of Cordina. It was like a miniature palace itself with its marble floors and carved columns. In the main lobby was a high, domed ceiling of stained glass and a circling balcony that gave the illusion of space.

Rooms ran off this circular hub like spokes of a wheel. On the floor below was a moderately priced restaurant where diners could enjoy a view of the gardens through a wide glass wall.

Hannah had arrived early to take inventory of the entire building. Security was tight but people who rested on the benches near the exhibits were largely ignored. Groups of school children were led by, most of them more impressed with an afternoon away from classes than they were with the paintings and sculptures. Tourists, brochures in hands, muddled through with a weaving of French, Italian, British, and American accents.

On a rainy weekday afternoon, the museum was a pleasant pastime. A healthy number of people flowed in and out. Hannah decided she couldn't have planned it better.

At the time she'd requested in her message, she strolled toward a Monet seascape. She loitered there long enough to read the plaque and study the brushwork. Whoever she was going to meet was probably there, making his own study of the building, and of her. In a leisurely pattern, she moved from painting to painting.

Then she saw the watercolor and both heart and mind raced back to the music room, and Bennett.

The plaque read Her Serene Highness, Princess Louisa de Cordina, but in small letters in the corner of the painting was the signature. Louisa Bisset.

She'd titled it simply *La Mer*. It was indeed the sea, but from a view Hannah had yet to see in Cordina. There was a jagged fall of cliffs that gave way to a sheer incline and ended in a jumble of rocks. From there, the beach spread white to the blue verge of water. But it wasn't peaceful. In this painting, the artist had looked for and captured the power and the danger. The spray rose high, and on the horizon a storm was brewing.

He found this stored in a trunk, Hannah thought and had to resist the urge to touch the frame as he might have done. He'd found it, she thought again, and perhaps had seen part of himself in it.

"An interesting subject."

The voice beside her was French, brusquely accented. Contact was made.

"Yes, the artist is very skillful." Hannah dropped her brochures. As she bent to pick them up she glanced around and was satisfied that no one was close enough to hear or even notice them. "I have information."

"You are to pass it through me."

She turned to smile at him as though they were exchanging a few pleasant remarks about the painting. He was of medium height, dark complexion with no scars. She gauged his age at fifty, though he might have been younger. Certain professions tend to age people quickly. He was not French by birth. The Germanic tone was faint, but she caught it and filed it away.

"There are certain aspects to some of my information that I feel must be given directly to the man who pays me."

"That is against the organization's policy."

"So I was told. However, I'm aware of what nearly happened six months ago because of policy. It wasn't looked on unfavorably when I used my own initiative and saved the organization, shall we say, certain embarrassments."

"*Mademoiselle*, I'm only here to receive your information."

"Then my information is this." Before speaking again, she moved toward another painting. Again, she took her time studying it. She lifted a hand as if to show her companion a certain combination of colors. "I have unlimited access to the palace. Neither my person nor my possessions are searched. I have already compiled the complete statistics on the security system both there and at the Fine Arts Center."

"That will be most useful."

"And will be given to the man who pays me. That is *my* policy, *monsieur*."

"You are paid by the organization."

"And the organization is run by men. I know who I work for and why." She turned to him then, her smile very cool, very calm. They might have been discussing the weather. "I am not a fool. The... organization has certain goals. So do I. I am more than happy to have them merge to our mutual satisfaction. I will meet and speak with the highest authority. See that it's soon.''

"Some people take a step and find themselves falling from a cliff.''

"I'm surefooted. Pass this on, *s'il vous plaît*. What I know is worth a great deal. What I can find out is worth even more. You'll find enough to prove it in here.'' Hannah let her brochure fall to her feet, but this time she left it there. *"Bonjour, monsieur."*

She turned, knowing that such demands would either take her to the next stage, or end in her being summarily disposed of. Nerves tingling, she began to wander toward the exit. Her heart stopped when Bennett walked in.

A dozen thoughts ran through her mind in a matter of seconds. Had she been set up? Had they used her to get him out in the open at a certain time and place? Had he come for her because Deboque had already struck somewhere else?

It took her only seconds more to dismiss them all as irrational. It was simply coincidence and bad luck that he should show up now on the tail of her meeting.

"I hope you don't mind company," Bennett said before she could think of a plausible opening.

"Of course not." She didn't dare look behind her yet to see if her contact was still there. She smiled, not quite sure how to behave since both she and Bennett had done an excellent job of avoiding each other for days. "The museum is even more beautiful than I'd been told."

"Have you seen everything? I'd be glad to show you around." He took her hand in a casual, friendly way that she realized could only cement her position if Deboque's man was watching.

She let her fingers curl into his, hating herself for using Bennett's generosity against him. "I could spend days looking, but I'm a bit tired."

She saw him then. He'd moved into her peripheral vision. The brochure she'd passed him was in his hand, and though his back was to them, she knew he was listening.

Bennett didn't notice the man, but only her. "Let me give you coffee up in my office. I'd like to talk with you."

She felt the unexpected prick of tears. Everything he said, and the way he said it, only made her claims more plausible. "I'd love some coffee." Hannah let him take her arm and lead her out, knowing every detail would be reported back to Deboque.

With a silent and stone-faced bodyguard, they stepped into an elevator. Bennett used a key to send them up to the third floor.

They crossed pale gray carpet, past uniformed guards to a suite of rooms. Two secretaries, one manning a bank of phones, the other working on a state-of-the-art computer, rose as Bennett entered.

"Janine, could we have some coffee, please?"

"Yes, Your Highness. Right away."

With his hand still on Hannah's arm, Bennett opened a door. The moment it shut behind them, the whispers started. His Highness had never brought a woman to his office before.

It was a room that reflected a man who loved beautiful things. Grays and blues blended softly with ivory walls. Deep-cushioned chairs invited long stays and easy conversation while an ornamental lemon tree thrived in a corner. Glass shelves held small treasures, a china bowl, a T'ang horse, a handful of shells she imagined he'd gathered himself and a chipped demitasse cup that might have been picked up in a flea market.

Though there was a very businesslike antique desk and chair, the essence of the room was relaxation. Hannah wondered if he came here when he needed to escape the palace and his title.

"Sit down, Hannah. If you've gone through the whole museum, you've been on your feet for hours."

"Yes, but I loved it." She chose a chair rather than the cozy lounge and folded her hands over each other on her lap. "I've always loved the Louvre, but this is so much more personal."

"The Board of Directors and the Chamber of Commerce will be delighted to hear it." He remained standing, his hands in his pockets, wondering just how to begin. "If you'd let me know you were coming today, I'd have enjoyed showing you through myself."

"I didn't want to disturb you. In any case, I rather liked just wandering."

Why, he's nervous, she realized. It might have pleased her in some secret place if she hadn't discovered she was nervous herself. It was the meeting, she told herself. No, it was Bennett. It was foolish to deny it.

"Do you work here often?"

"When necessary. It's often more convenient to work out of my office at home." He didn't want to talk about the museum. Bennett dug his hands deeper in his pockets. Since when had he had trouble talking to a woman? Since Hannah, he thought wryly, and tried again. "Hannah—"

The knock on the door had him biting off an oath. Bennett opened the door for Janine and the coffee tray. The pot was silver, Hannah noted, while the cups were violet bone china edged in gold.

"Yes, just set it down there, Janine. I'll see to it."

"Yes, sir." She set it down on the table in front of the lounge then curtsied.

Aware he'd been terse, Bennett smiled at her. "Thank you, Janine. It smells wonderful."

"You're welcome, sir." The door closed behind her with a discreet click.

"Looks like we're in luck." Bennett lifted the pot and poured. "These little pastries are from the restaurant downstairs. They're wonderful. Cream?"

"Yes, thank you. No sugar." How polite we are, she thought as the tension began to spread from her neck to her shoulders. Like two strangers on a blind date.

"Will you come sit over here if I promise to behave?"

Though he said it lightly, Hannah heard the strain. She lowered her gaze to her hands. He couldn't know it was shame and not shyness. "Of course." Rising, she moved over and joined him on the lounge. She lifted her coffee while he left his alone.

"Hannah, I apologize for my behavior the other night. It's no wonder you were offended."

"Oh, please, don't." With a distress even her training couldn't smother, she set her cup down and started to rise. His hand reached for hers and held her still. "I don't want an apology." Fighting for control, she forced herself to look at him. "I wasn't offended, really. I was just—"

"Frightened then? That's just as inexcusable."

"No—yes." Which answer was the right one? In the end, she gave up. "Bennett, the truest thing I can say to you is that no one has ever confused me so well."

"Thank you."

"That wasn't a compliment, but a complaint."

"Hannah, thank God you're back." Laughing, he pulled both her hands to his lips. When she stiffened, he released them but continued to smile.

"Friends?"

Still wary, she nodded. "I'd like to be."

"Then friends it is." Satisfied the first hurdle was successfully negotiated, Bennett sat back. He would wait and be a great deal more cautious before attempting the second. "What did you like best about the museum?"

She didn't trust him. No, Hannah was far too good at game playing not to know when one was afoot. "The airy, unrestricted atmosphere, I think. Too often museums are solemn, serious places. Oh, I did see another of your ancestor's paintings. The one of the sea. It was stunning."

"One of my favorites." He was careful not to touch her again. "I was tempted to keep it locked in my room, all to myself, but..." With a shrug he picked up his cup. "It didn't seem fair."

"And you are fair," she murmured, knowing she'd used him.

"I try to be," he returned, knowing he would use fair means or foul to win her. "Hannah, you ride, don't you?"

"Yes."

"Ride with me tomorrow morning. It has to be early as the rest of my day is full, but it's been a long time since I had any company on a ride."

"I'm not sure I can. Eve—"

"Will be busy with Marissa until ten," Bennett finished.

How she would love a ride. An hour of freedom and movement. "Yes, but I've promised to go with her to the Center. She has appointments there at eleven."

"We'll be back by then if you're willing to start out early." He wasn't willing to lose the opportunity. In her eyes he saw hesitation and pressed his advantage. "Come, Cordina's at its best in the morning on horseback."

"All right then." It was impulse, she knew, but she could use an hour of relaxation.

In a matter of days, she would meet with Deboque. Hannah lifted her coffee again and sipped. Or she would be dead.

Chapter Six

He hadn't lied. Hannah had already thought Cordina beautiful, but in the early morning it was exquisite. With the dawn light, Cordina reminded Hannah of a young girl dressing for her first ball. The colors were soft, shimmering. Pinks and roses and misty blues still gathered to the east as they got mounted.

Settling into her own saddle, Hannah eyed Bennett's Dracula with a mixture of envy and anxiety. Her father's stables included some of the finest horseflesh in Britain, but he had nothing to compare with the black stallion. He looked fast and reckless and just a bit angry. Even as she imagined herself on his back, she could also picture Bennett being thrown.

"A mount like that would have a mind of his own," she commented when the old groom stepped back from the prince.

"Of course." Bennett steadied the stallion as he sidestepped. Then, misunderstanding her, he smiled in reassurance. "Your Quixote's strong, but quite the gentleman. Brie often rides him when she's here."

Hannah only lifted a brow, recognizing the soothing words for what they were. "Thank you, sir. It eases my mind to know you've given me a lady's mount."

He thought he caught a trace of sarcasm, but when he looked at her he saw only calm eyes and a polite smile. "I thought we'd ride to the sea."

"I'd like that."

With a nod, Bennett turned his horse and started off at a gentle trot. "Are you comfortable?"

"Yes, thank you." As she settled into the easy rhythm, Hannah tried not to yearn for a wild gallop. "It was kind of you to invite me. I'm told your morning rides are sacred."

He grinned at her, pleased that she sat the horse well and confidently. "It's often true that I need an hour on horseback before I can be civil. Still, there are times I prefer company."

That hadn't been true lately. Since Deboque's release he felt he could never stretch his arms out without bumping a guard. And still nothing. His eyes clouded, as much with impatience as with anger. He wanted Deboque to move. He relished the thought of being able to deal with him personally, and finally. Instinctively he touched a hand to his shoulder where a bullet had entered. Yes, he would relish it.

The look in his eyes made her uneasy. There was something to watch for and defend against there. The man beside her was not the easygoing, easy loving prince she'd come to expect. Whatever, whoever he thought of seemed to communicate itself to his mount for Dracula shied nervously. She saw how easily he controlled the stallion, only a flexing of muscle. He could be kind or harsh, gentle or rough. Her own palm grew damp on the reins.

"Is something wrong?"

"What?" He glanced over. For an instant the look was still there, hard and dark enough to make her tense. Then it was gone and he was smiling again. There was no Deboque this morning, Bennett told himself. He was sick of having every aspect of his life and his family's lives clouded by one name. "No, nothing. Tell me what you do at home, Hannah. I can't picture you there."

"We live quietly in London." It was partially the truth. She wondered why she thought of it as partially a lie. "I do a great deal of my work at home, which makes it convenient for me to keep house for my father."

"Your work," he repeated. "Your essays?" He was leading her along the easiest route, where the incline was gentle.

"Yes." Again, there was a twinge of discomfort. "I hope to have them ready for publication in a year or two."

"I'd like to read them."

She shot him a look of surprise, then almost immediately felt her muscles tighten. It had nothing to do with fear. Even if he'd demanded to see her work, she had enough that would satisfy him. No, it wasn't fear but a certainty that if she had to continue to lie to him much longer, she would be physically ill.

"You're welcome to, of course, but I don't think my writing would be of great interest to you."

"You're wrong. You're of great interest to me."

She looked down, but not in the shyness he thought he saw. Once again it was shame. "It's lovely here," she managed after a moment. "Do you ride this way often?"

She wouldn't allow him to get too close. Bennett fought back frustration and reminded himself he was in for the long haul. "No, actually I haven't been this way in quite a while." When they reached the top of a rise, he stopped. Her gelding was content to busy himself with the grass alongside the path. Beside her, Dracula nearly shivered with energy. She thought she felt the same impatience from Bennett.

"A little distance changes things," he murmured.

Following his gaze, she looked back at the palace. From here it looked like an exquisite child's toy, a magnificent dollhouse a pampered child might find near the tree on Christmas morning. To the east was the sea, still hidden from view by the cliffs and trees and barely heard. Like the palace, it hardly seemed real.

"Do you need to get away from it so badly?" Hannah asked him quietly.

"Sometimes." It no longer surprised him that she read his moods. With a hand firm on the reins, he controlled the stallion and continued to look at his home. "I had my time at Oxford, and at sea. When I was away, I missed Cordina so badly it was like an ache. In the past six months, year, I've felt a restlessness, a waiting for something to happen."

They both thought of Deboque.

"Often in England, especially at this time of year, I'll complain about the cold and the damp." She shifted in the saddle then smiled as she thought of her home. "I'll look out the window and think I'd almost sell my soul for a week of warm, sunny days. Then, when I'm away, I begin to miss the fog and the mists and the smells of London."

They began to walk the horses again while she cast her mind back to England. "There's a man who sells roasted chestnuts just around the corner from our house. You can buy a little bag and warm your hands on them and smell them, just smell them long before you ever eat them." Remembering made her smile again, but she had no idea how wistfully. "Sometimes I'd wonder how it could be Christmastime anywhere without roasted chestnuts."

"I didn't know you missed England so much."

Nor had she until that moment. "One always misses home. Our hearts are always there." And what she was, all that she had done, had always been for England first.

"I've often wondered how difficult it was for Reeve," Bennett said. The sounds of the sea became louder as they moved their way east. "Although he and Brie spend nearly six months every year at their farm in America. I know for Brie it's as much home as Cordina is."

"For many, real contentment comes with acclimation." Hadn't it been so for her, all of her adult life?

"It's a great deal harder for Eve. She has only a few weeks with her family in America."

"Some loves are greater than others. Some needs stronger." She was just beginning to truly understand it. "Eve would live anywhere as long as Alexander was with her. And I think the same is true for your brother-in-law."

Yes, it was true. Perhaps that was a part of the restlessness in him. Over the last few years he'd seen how beautiful, how strong, real commitment, real feelings could be. Somehow they always seemed so remote from him, so unattainable. Now there was Hannah.

"For love, could you turn your back on England?"

Hannah caught her first glimpse of the sea as they climbed higher. She concentrated on that, but saw, in her mind's eyes, the twisting charm of the Thames.

Could she? So much of her life, so much of her duty was bound with England. Even her current assignment had been as much to protect her country from Deboque as it had been to insure the safety of the Royal Family of Cordina.

"I don't know. You especially would understand how strong some ties can be."

The trees thinned. Those that remained were bent and battered from the wind that swept in from the sea. The path grew rougher so that Bennett put himself between the edge and Hannah. Her mouth twitched at the move, but she said nothing. He could hardly know that she was capable of riding down the path pell-mell without saddle or reins. Besides, she found herself savoring the unaccustomed feeling of being protected.

Without the trees to break its power, the wind swirled from the sea to the top of the rise, carrying traces of salt. Even Hannah's tightly pinned hair couldn't resist it completely. Wispy tendrils escaped to dance around her cheeks. As she watched, a gull caught the current and glided peacefully up on a stream of air. Another, far below, skimmed the water looking for food.

"It's breathtaking." She relaxed enough to sigh.

He saw what was always in her heart, but which showed so rarely in her eyes. Her love of adventure, of power and of risk. It made her beautiful, arousing, mysterious. The need to reach out for her was so strong, he had to tighten his fingers on the reins to keep them still.

"I wanted to bring you here, but I worried that the height might bother you."

"No, I love it." Her horse shied a bit and she controlled him with the ease of long experience. "There are so many beautiful places in the world, but so few special ones. This is a special one. I think I could..." She trailed off as the full impact struck her. "This is the scene from the painting. There's no storm brewing, but this is it, isn't it?"

"Yes." He had no idea that her recognition of it would mean so much. Nor did he know what to do with the sudden, inescapable realization that he was in love with her. Completely. Unalterably.

He tossed his head back as the wind blew his hair into his eyes. He wanted a clear look at her, at this, perhaps the most important moment in his life.

She sat straight in the saddle, her eyes dark with appreciation of the scene spread out before and below them. Her profile was sharp, sculpted. The plain brown riding skirt and pants did nothing to enhance her pale skin. But when he looked at her, he saw the most beautiful, the most precious thing he'd ever found. And for the first time in his life, he had no words to tell her.

"Hannah." He reached out a hand and waited.

She turned. He was the most magnificent man she'd ever seen. More breathtaking than the view, more dangerous than a plunge to the rocks below. He sat on the huge stallion, straight as a soldier, as heartbreaking as a poet. In his eyes she saw both passion and compassion, both need and generosity.

Her heart betrayed her and was lost to him even before she could tell herself it couldn't be. As duty warred with emotion, she let her hand join with his.

"I know what you think I am."

"Bennett—"

"No." His fingers tightened on hers. "You're not far wrong. I could lie to you and promise to change, but I won't lie or promise."

Before she could stop herself, she softened. Only for this moment, she promised herself. There was magic, if only for the moment.

"Bennett, I don't want you to change."

"I meant what I said, though I said it badly the other night. I do want you, Hannah." Like her, he looked out to sea. "I also understand that it would be difficult for you to believe that I've never said that to another woman and meant it in the same way."

But she did believe him. It was thrilling, terrifying and forbidden, but she did. For one glorious moment, she let herself hope. Then she remembered who she was. Duty was first. Always.

"Please, believe me, if I could give you what you want, I would. It's just not possible." She drew her hand away because the contact was making her weak, making her dream.

"I've always believed anything is possible if you work hard enough for it."

"No, some things remain out of reach." She turned her horse away from the sea. "We should get back."

Before she could move, he'd backed up enough to cover the hands on her reins with his own. His arm brushed her arm, his leg, her leg. His face was close, too close, as their mounts stood in opposite directions.

"Tell me what you feel," he demanded. The patience was gone, dissolved in need and frustration. "Give me that much, dammit."

"Regret." As she spoke, the word shimmered with it.

He released her hands only to cup the back of her neck. "Tell me again how you feel," he murmured, then leaned toward her.

The kiss was like a whisper, soft, seductive, sultry. Hannah tightened her hands on the reins, then let them go limp as emotion swamped her. It wasn't supposed to be like this, so encompassing, so heady, so right. The wind ribboned around them. The sea crashed below. For a moment, just one moment, all rational thought fled, leaving only desires behind.

"Bennett." She only murmured his name as she started to draw away. He held her, firm, insistent.

"Another moment."

He needed it. He needed every scrap she would throw him. Never had he felt the desire to beg for what a woman could give or withhold. It wasn't just the passion he wanted; it was more than the physical. He wanted her heart with a desperation he'd never felt before.

It was that desperation that made him keep the kiss gentle, that made him draw back long before his craving for her was satisfied. If he wanted her heart, he would have to move slowly. His Hannah was delicate and shy.

"No regrets, Hannah," he said quietly, then smiled. "I won't hurt you, or push you further than you're ready for. Trust me. That's really all I want for now."

She wanted to weep. He was giving her a kindness, a sensitivity she didn't deserve. Lies were all she'd given him. Lies were all she would continue to give. To keep him alive, she reminded herself as the tears burned at the back of her eyes. To keep him and the people he loved safe and unharmed.

"No regrets," she told him, letting the words echo through her mind for herself. Tossing her head, she pressed her heels to the gelding's sides and took off in a gallop.

Bennett's first reaction was surprise. He hadn't expected her to ride so well or so forcefully. He took a moment to watch her race down the rise before he grinned and let Dracula have his head. Though she'd taken a good lead, Hannah heard them gaining ground behind her. Delighted, she bent lower over the gelding's neck as she urged him on.

"We can't beat them head-to-head," she called to her mount. "But we might outwit them."

The challenge was enough. Spurred by it, Hannah swung off the track and into the trees. The path here was narrow and rough, but what she sacrificed in speed, she gained in maneuverability. Bennett was hard on her heels, but she kept to the center giving him no room to pass. She burst through the trees and onto a field less than two lengths ahead. Instinct had her veering to the left and pounding up another rise so that Bennett had to check his momentum at the unexpected maneuver. Still, he continued to gain so that when the stables came into view they were nearly neck and neck. Laughing, she veered left again and headed for a hedge.

He felt an instant's panic as he imagined her flying off her mount onto the ground. Then they were sailing over, side by side. Heels down, knees snug, they thundered toward the stables.

Pipit stood with his hands on his hips. He'd watched them since they'd barreled over the rise with the gelding in the lead. Since they'd taken the jump, the stallion had pulled ahead with smooth, easy strides. To be expected, Pipit thought as he rubbed his hands on the thighs of his pants. There wasn't another horse in Cordina—or in Europe as far as he was concerned—that could match the stallion.

But he thought as he watched the woman keep the distance close that Prince Bennett had at last met his match.

Bennett reined in and slid from the horse's back with excitement still drumming in his head. She was only seconds behind him. Her laughter was low and a bit breathless as she started to swing down. Bennett was there to take her by the waist and turn her to him before her feet hit the ground.

"How did you learn to ride like that?"

She lifted her hands to his chest, as much to keep the distance as her balance. "It's the one thing I excel at other than literature. I'd forgotten how much I've missed it these last few months."

He couldn't take his eyes off her. It was pure desire now, basic, vital. The ride they could have together would be as wild, as reckless as the ride they'd just completed. Somehow he knew it, could almost taste it. For reasons he couldn't name, he felt that he was holding two women. One the calm, one the passionate. He wasn't sure which one drew him more.

"Ride with me tomorrow."

Once had been a risk and a delight. Twice, Hannah knew, would be a foolish mistake. "I don't think that's possible. With Eve's play about to open, there's so much to be done at the theater."

He wouldn't push. He'd promised himself that he would give her the time to become accustomed to having him with her. From the moment on the rise when he'd realized just what that meant to him, he'd been more determined than ever to court her properly.

A first for the Royal Rake, he thought as he stepped back to kiss her hand.

"The stables are at your disposal whenever you find the time to use them."

"I appreciate that." She reached up a hand to her hair to be certain her pins were in place. "I enjoyed this, Bennett, very much."

"So did I."

"Well, Eve will be waiting for me."

"Go ahead. Pipit and I will see to them."

"Thank you." She was stalling. The moment she realized it, Hannah drew herself in. "Goodbye, Bennett."

"Hannah." He nodded, then watched her walk back toward the palace. A smile tugged at his mouth as he patted his horse's neck. "I'm getting to her, *mon ami*," he murmured. "It's just going to take a bit of time."

Time moved so quickly. Locked in her room, Hannah held the letter from Sussex. Inside, she would find Deboque's answer to the demand she'd made only days before in the museum. Her hands were steady as she sat at her desk. With the ivory-handled letter opener provided her, she slit through the envelope. Inside was a casual, even uninspired letter from an acquaintance in England. It took Hannah less than fifteen minutes to decode it.

Request granted. December third, 23:30. Café du Dauphin. Alone. Contact will ask for the time, in English, then comment, in French, on the weather. Be certain your information warrants the exception to procedure.

Tonight. The next step would be taken tonight. Hannah folded the letter back into the envelope, but left it in plain view on her desk. Beside it was a single white rose Bennett had sent to her that morning. Hannah hesitated, then gave herself the pleasure of touching the petals.

If only life were as sweet and as simple.

Moments later, she was knocking on Prince Armand's office door.

It was opened by his secretary who bowed stiffly to her before announcing her to the prince. Armand stood behind his desk as he gave permission to admit her.

"Your Highness." Hannah made a deep curtsy. "I apologize for disturbing you."

"Not at all, Hannah."

"But you're busy." She stood just inside of the door, hands folded. "I only wished to ask your advice on something. If it's convenient, I'll come back later."

"It's convenient now. Please come in and sit. Michel, if you would see to those few matters now, I'll have a private word with Lady Hannah."

"Of course, Your Highness." Michel bowed his way out of the room. When the door was closed, Hannah dropped her hands to her sides. Her stride firm, she walked to the desk. "We've gotten a break. You'll have to call Reeve immediately."

"I'm not easy about this," Armand said some time later when his son-in-law sat across from him. "How can we be sure Deboque will be fooled by the information Hannah will feed him?"

"Because it's so nearly the truth." Reeve downed his second cup of coffee. "Unless Hannah can give him something important, something he has no other way of getting, she'll never get close to him."

"But will he believe her?"

"It's my job to make sure he does," Hannah said quietly. "Your Highness, I know you've had objections to this operation all along, but up to this point it's worked exactly as we've wanted."

"To this point," Armand agreed, and rose. He gestured them both back into their seats so that he could pace in peace. "Now I'm in the position of asking a woman, a woman who both my family and myself have become very fond of, to go alone to meet a man who kills as much for pleasure as for profit."

"She won't be alone."

At Reeve's announcement, Hannah sat straight up. "I have to be. If Deboque or one of his men have the slightest clue that I'm not, the whole operation goes up in smoke. I won't have it." Now, she rose as well. "I've given this two years of my life."

"And I intend to see that you live a bit longer," Reeve said mildly. "We suspect that Deboque has his headquarters in a small villa about five miles from here. We'll have men watching it."

"And they'll have Deboque's men watching them."

"Leave that part to me, Hannah, and do your job. You have the blueprints and the specs on the security systems?"

"Yes, of course." Annoyed, she sat again. "And I know I'm to give them to no one but Deboque."

"You also know that at the first sign that things are going wrong, you're to pull out."

She nodded, though she had no intention of doing so. "Yes."

"There'll be two men stationed at the café."

"Why don't you just send up a flare?" Hannah tossed back.

He understood her frustration, but merely poured a third cup of coffee. "It's a choice between that or wiring you."

"The last agent who attempted to get a wire into Deboque's organization was sent back to the ISS in three boxes."

Reeve moved his shoulders. "Your choice."

Again, Hannah rose. "I'm not used to being second-guessed, Reeve." When he said nothing, she set her teeth. "I realize that you're my superior on this assignment, so I don't believe I have much of a choice."

"As long as we understand each other." He rose then, and took her hand. "Hannah, I'm aware of your reputation. Why don't we just say I don't want to take any chances on losing one of the best?" Releasing her, he turned back to the prince. "I have a few things to put into motion. I'll keep in touch."

Armand waited until the door was closed again. "Another moment, please," he said to Hannah. "If you'd sit?"

She wanted to be alone, to plan each detail out carefully. There was only a matter of hours left. Breeding was as strong as training, so she sat. "Would you like me to go over things with you again, sir?"

"No." His lips curved, just slightly. "I believe I grasp the situation well enough. I have a personal question, Hannah, and I ask you beforehand not to be offended." He sat across from her, militarily straight. "Am I mistaken, or has my son become fond of you?"

She linked her hands together immediately as her whole body went on alert. "If you mean Prince Bennett, sir, he's been very kind."

"Hannah, for my sake, please dispense with the evasions and the manners. Too often duty has interfered with the time I can spend with my family, but that doesn't mean I don't know my children and know them well. I believe Bennett is in love with you."

She went pale instantly. "No." She had to swallow, but the word came out a second time just as strongly. "No, he's not. Perhaps he's a bit intrigued, but only because I'm not the kind of woman he's used to spending time with."

"Hannah." Armand held up a hand before she could continue her rambling denial. "I don't ask in order to upset you. When I began to suspect this, it made me uncomfortable only because Bennett is unaware of your true purpose here."

"I understand."

"I'm not sure you do. Bennett is more like his mother than my other children. So... kindhearted. His temper has more of a lash, but his feelings are more easily reached. I only ask you this because if the answer to my next question is no, I must request that you tread softly. Do you love him, Hannah?"

Everything she felt was in her eyes. She knew it, and lowered her gaze quickly. "Whatever I feel for Bennett, for your family, won't interfere with my job."

"I know enough to recognize a person who will do what has to be done." He felt a stirring for her, a grave kind of pity that twined with empathy. "But you didn't answer me. Do you love my son?"

"I can't." This time her voice wasn't strong and there were tears chasing behind it. "I've lied to him since the first, and I'll go on doing so. You can't love and lie. Please excuse me, Your Highness."

Armand let her go. For a moment, he sat back in the chair and closed his eyes. For the next few hours, he could do nothing more than pray for her.

The café wasn't one of the pretty little tourist spots in Cordina. It was a local waterfront bar that catered to the crews from the fishing and cargo boats. Inside it was cramped with tables, many empty, and smoke and the smell of liquor. Not as rough as they came, Hannah thought as she slipped inside, but neither was it a place where a woman alone would wander unless she was looking for trouble.

Still, she didn't cause much of a stir as she came in. In her plain gray sweater and slacks, she nearly blended into the walls. The handful of women who were already there were more interesting fare. If she could get this over with quickly, she might not have to discourage any of the locals.

Hannah chose a bar stool and ordered a bourbon, neat. By the time it was served, she had sized up the room. If Reeve had indeed planted two agents here, they were certainly good ones. It was a rare thing when Hannah couldn't spot one of her own.

She'd been drinking silently for ten minutes when one of the men stood from a table and wandered in her direction.

Hannah continued to drink while every muscle tensed. When he spoke, it was in French and thickened by whiskey.

"It's a sad thing for a woman to drink alone."

Hannah relaxed only enough to be annoyed. She used her primmest British tones. "It's a sadder thing for a woman not to remain alone when she chooses to."

"When one is so plain, she shouldn't be so picky," he grumbled, but moved away again. Hannah nearly smiled, then another man came through the doors.

He was dressed in seaman's clothes, with his cap pulled low. Beneath it his face was deeply tanned and gaunt. This time she tensed because she was certain.

Still, she idly lifted her drink as he moved to sit beside her at the bar.

"You have the time, *mademoiselle*?"

"Yes, it's quarter to twelve."

"Thank you." He signaled for a drink. Another minute passed as he toyed with it. *"Il fait chaud ce soir."*

"Oui, un peu."

They didn't speak again. Behind them a group began to sing a song, in French and off-key. The wine was flowing freely and the night was still young. He finished his drink and left the bar. Hannah waited only a moment, then got up to follow.

He waited for her at the edge of the dock. There was little lighting here so that he was more shadow than man. Hannah moved toward him, knowing it could be the beginning or the end for her.

"You have the information." Again he spoke in English. It was bland and unaccented, just as his French had been. Deboque chose well, she thought and only nodded.

"We go by boat." He indicated the small open runabout.

Hannah knew she had no choice. She could refuse, or she could go on. Though she knew she would have no backup on the sea, she never even considered the first. Deboque was the destination. That was the bottom line.

Without hesitation, she lowered herself into the boat and took a seat at the stern. In silence, her contact got in beside her, cast off, and started the engine. It sounded like thunder on the open water.

Hannah took a deep breath. She was on her way.

Chapter Seven

Reeve would be furious. Hannah rested a hand on the seat for balance as the boat picked up speed. He could afford to be, she thought, but she had to keep her head.

So Deboque wasn't on land in the villa as they'd expected. He was, unless the boat made a sudden and dramatic change in direction, at sea. No, there would be no backup now. Hannah drew another deep breath and watched the water wake behind them. She preferred working alone in any case.

Tonight, she would meet Deboque. She could feel it. Her pulse was slow and steady, her breathing even. The spray the boat kicked up teased her skin as she kept her expression placid. Nerves, what there were of them, couldn't be allowed to show. Her midnight cruise across the Mediterranean was bringing her closer to the goal she'd worked toward for just over twenty-four months.

Excitement, not fear, was building inside of her. Even that had to be controlled. Anything that made the pulse beat too fast or tempted the mind to swing too far ahead was dangerous. She couldn't make a mistake. Over the past two years she'd worked her way up in Deboque's organization, relying for the most part on her own skill. With the backing of the ISS she'd seen several jobs through to completion. Arms sold, diamonds liberated, drugs delivered.

The end justifies the means.

Rungs on the ladder, she thought. If she could continue to climb, it wouldn't be long before Deboque's kingdom of misery would come tumbling down on his own shoulders.

The trickiest rung had been making the well-placed Bouffe look incompetent. Deboque's senior lieutenant wasn't a fool and it'd taken a lot of guile and some risk to see that several of his assignments over the last few months had fallen through, without throwing suspicion back on herself. The biggest of these had been the arms deal with a terrorist group known for their lack of patience.

It had been sticky, but the timing had been perfect. Hannah had managed to make it seem as though Bouffe had nearly botched the deal before she had slipped in to make things right.

The terrorists had their arms—she had to leave the ISS to deal with that. And Deboque had his five million francs. It would be her pleasure to deal with that. And soon.

She saw the sleek white yacht anchored majestically in dark water. A thrill of anticipation moved through her. At the wheel, her contact signaled with an electric lantern. There was an answering flash from the ship. The engine was cut, throwing the night into silence as they drifted alongside the yacht.

Hannah reached out for the ladder and found the metal cool and hard. She knew she would be the same. Without a backward glance, she climbed up, and into the unknown.

"Lady Hannah."

There was a tall, dark-skinned man waiting for her. He took her hand and bowed over it. She recognized him from her last briefing, though she would have placed his accent as Jamaican in any case. He was Ricardo Batemen, a twenty-six-year-old islander, an ivy-league graduate with a degree in medicine. He still used a scalpel, but he preferred to wield in on the healthy and unanesthetized.

He had become a favorite of Deboque's.

"I'm Ricardo." His young, smooth face spread into a smile. "Welcome to the *Invincible*."

"Thank you, Ricardo." She gave a casual look around and counted five more men and one woman on deck. The men were dressed in dark suits and carried machine guns. The woman had a sarong draped over a bikini and looked bored. "Might I have a drink?"

"Of course." His eyes, she noted, were pale, an almost translucent green that never seemed to blink. His voice was like rich cream over hot coffee. "But first, you must excuse our precautions. Your bag, Lady Hannah."

She lifted a brow and met his eyes straight on. "I'll depend on you to see that everything in it is returned to me."

"You have my word." He bowed as she handed it to him. "Now, if you would go with Carmine. She will take you to your cabin. You may like to freshen up after she makes certain no one has planted any electronic devices on you."

A strip search, Hannah thought resignedly. "No one plants anything on me, Ricardo. But I admire a cautious man." Hannah crossed the deck to Carmine as though she was going to tea.

Moments later, Ricardo set Hannah's black alligator bag on a gleaming mahogany desk. "Carmine is seeing to her. She has a small-caliber pistol, her passport and identification and about three thousand francs along with a few cosmetics. There is an envelope, sealed."

"Thank you, Ricardo." The voice was deep and smoky with its traces of France. "You may bring her to me in ten minutes. Then we won't be disturbed."

"Oui, monsieur."

"Ricardo, your impressions?"

"Attractive enough, more so than her photograph. And cool, very cool. Her hand was dry and steady."

"Good." There was a trace of amusement in the voice now. "Ten minutes, Ricardo." He picked up the envelope and broke the seal.

A short time later, Hannah adjusted her sweater. She'd found the search more annoying than humiliating. Carmine had taken her stiletto, but she'd expected that. Ricardo had her pistol. For now, she was alone and unarmed in the middle of the sea. She still had her wits.

Hannah stood in the center of the cabin when Ricardo opened the door. "My apologies again for the inconvenience, Lady Hannah."

"A small annoyance, Ricardo." He hadn't brought back her bag, but she said nothing of it. "I hope there won't be too many more."

"None at all. If you'd just come with me."

Hannah followed him, walking easily as the boat swayed in the current. It was the size of a small hotel, she'd noted. And there were escape routes if it became necessary. The carpet they walked on was rich red. In the cabin where she'd been searched had been an antique mirror with beveled glass and a bedspread in velvet. There had also been a porthole big enough for a child, or a slender woman to work their way through.

Ricardo stopped by a glossy oak door and knocked twice. Without waiting for an answer, he turned the knob and gestured her inside. Hannah stepped through and heard the door click shut at her back.

It was opulent, elegant, even fanciful. Eighteenth-century France seemed to come alive. Now the carpet was the deep shimmering blue of kings and the paneled walls were polished to a mirrorlike gleam. Two delicate, glittering chandeliers sprinkled light over the antique wood and plush upholstery. Brocade had been used lavishly to drape over and around a bed fit for a king. All the colors were vivid, almost shocking.

There was a scent of something floral and something old that merged together into one strangely compelling and oddly uneasy fragrance. With the gentle sway of the ship, a collection of crystal animals shuddered with life.

It only took Hannah seconds to absorb this. As grand and extravagant as the room was, the man who sat behind the Louis XVI desk dominated. She didn't feel the evil she'd expected to. With the truly wicked, Hannah knew you often experienced a chill or a dread. What she saw was a slender and attractive man in his fifties, with steel-gray hair flowing back in a mane from a chiseled, aristocratic face. He wore black. It seemed to accent his almost poetically-pale skin. His eyes were black, too, like a raven's. They studied her now as his full, rather beautiful mouth curved into a smile.

She'd seen pictures of him, of course. She'd studied every scrap of information that had been gathered on him in the last twenty years. And yet... And yet she hadn't been prepared for the shock of sensuality which seemed to emanate from him.

He was a man women had died for. And now she understood it. He was a man whom other men had killed for without question. She understood that, too, as she stood ten feet away and felt the power.

"Lady Hannah." He rose, slowly, gracefully. His body was trim, almost delicate. His hand, as he offered it to her, was narrow and beautiful with a trio of diamonds on long fingers.

She couldn't hesitate, though she felt if her hand touched his she would be pulled out of what she knew into something foreign and frightening.

Hannah smiled and stepped forward. "Monsieur Deboque." She was glad to see his slight surprise at her use of his name. "It's a pleasure."

"Please sit. Will you have brandy?"

"Yes, thank you." She chose a soft high-backed chair that faced the desk. There was music playing through hidden speakers. Chopin. She listened to the notes as Deboque crossed to an enameled cabinet and withdrew a decanter. "Your ship is exquisite, *monsieur*." There was a painting behind his desk. One of six she knew had been stolen from a private collection only the year before. She herself had helped execute the theft.

"I appreciate beauty." He offered the brandy, then instead of going behind the desk again, sat beside her. "To your health, *mademoiselle*."

"And yours." She smiled at him again before she sipped.

"Perhaps you will tell me how you became aware of my name."

"I make it a habit of knowing who I work for, Monsieur Deboque." She shook her head as he drew out a cigarette case and offered her one. "I must congratulate you on your security and your staff. Discovering who, shall we say, reigned, was hardly an easy matter."

He drew in the smoke slowly, as a man who appreciated fine tastes. "Most have found it impossible."

Her eyes were cool and amused on his. "I find little impossible."

"Others have found it fatal." When she only smiled, he let it pass. She was, as Ricardo had said, very cool. "My reports on you are very flattering, Lady Hannah."

"Of course."

It was his turn to smile. "I admire confidence."

"And I."

"It appears I'm in your debt for smoothing over an exchange with our Mediterranean neighbors a few months ago. I would have been, to say the least, annoyed to have lost that contract."

"It was my pleasure. It would seem, *monsieur*, that you have a few weak links in the chain."

"It would seem," he murmured. He'd already debated handing Bouffe over to Ricardo for disposal. A pity, Deboque thought. Bouffe had been a loyal and valued employee for over a decade. "You are enjoying your stay in Cordina?"

Her heart drummed lightly but she sipped again. "The palace is quite lovely." She moved her shoulders as she let her gaze roam around the room. "I, too, appreciate beauty. It helps compensate for the fact that the Bissets are a bit boring."

"You're not impressed with the Royal Family, Lady Hannah?"

"I'm not easily impressed. They are certainly very pretty people, but so...devoted." She tinted her voice with derision, lightly. "I prefer devoting myself to something more tangible than honor and duty."

"And loyalty, Lady Hannah?"

She turned to him again. He was looking deep, trying to see inside, trying to see beyond. "I can be loyal." She touched her tongue to the rim of her snifter. "As long as it's profitable."

It was a chance, she knew. Disloyalty in Deboque's organization was punishable by death. She waited, outwardly cool while a single line of sweat beaded down her back. He studied her a moment, then threw his lion's head back and laughed. Hannah felt each individual muscle in her body sing with relief.

"An honest woman. I admire that. Yes, I admire that a great deal more than sworn oaths." He drew in the rich French smoke then exhaled again. "It would seem to my advantage to continue to make it profitable for someone of your skills and ambitions."

"I was hoping you'd see it that way. I prefer the executive branch, if you comprehend, Monsieur Deboque, but I'm willing to work my way to it. Delegation, organization, is so much more rewarding than execution, don't you think?''

"Indeed, yes." He studied her again, considering. She appeared to be a mild, well-bred young woman of some means. He preferred a quiet, unassuming outer shell in a woman. He thought briefly of Janet Smithers who he'd used and discarded nearly a decade before. Lady Hannah, he thought, might prove to be a great deal more interesting, and more competent. "You've been with us two years now?"

"Yes."

"And in those two years, you've proven yourself to be very useful." He rose now and retrieved the envelope on his desk. "You brought this to me, I assume?"

"I did." She swirled her brandy. "Though I found the method with which it was delivered irksome."

"My apologies. This information is interesting, Lady Hannah, but I fear, incomplete."

She crossed her legs and relaxed back in the chair. "A woman who writes everything she knows on paper loses her value quickly. What isn't there, is in here." She laid a finger against her temple.

"I see." He admired an employee who knew her own worth, and guarded it. "If we say I'm interested in the security systems of the Royal Palace, the Fine Arts Center, the museum, for the purpose of emulating such systems for my own use, you would be able to fill in the blanks?"

"Of course."

"And if I asked how you came by such information?"

"This was the purpose of my visit to Cordina."

"One of them." Intrigued, he tapped the envelope on his palm. "It was fortunate that you were able to become close to Princess Eve."

"Fortunate, but not difficult. She was lonely for female companionship. I'm accommodating. I fuss over her daughter, listen to her fears and complaints. By easing some of her workload, I also earn the gratitude of Prince Alexander. He worries that his wife will tire herself while carrying his child.''

"And you are trusted?''

"Implicitly. And why not?'' she added. "My family is well respected, my breeding without mark. Prince Armand sees me as a young cousin of his dead wife. Your pardon, *monsieur*, but aren't these the reasons you enlisted me to find a place at the palace?''

"Yes, they are.'' He sat back. She pleased him, but he was a long way from giving her his full confidence. "I have word that the young prince is interested in you.''

Something inside her froze at that. "Your network of information is admirable.'' Hannah glanced at her empty snifter, then tilted it in question. Deboque rose immediately to refill her glass. It was just enough time to regain her composure.

"Bennett is, as I'm sure you're aware, invariably interested in the female closest at hand.'' She gave a low laugh and tried not to hate herself. "He's really only a boy, and spoiled at that. I've found the simplest way to handle him is to act disinterested.''

Deboque nodded slowly. "Then he pursues.''

"Such men are always more—accommodating under those circumstances.''

"I beg your pardon if I seem to be getting too personal, my dear, but how accommodating?''

"He's a bit bored, a bit reckless. His weakness for women should have its uses. I believe with a certain—flair—information can be drawn out of him. It was he, you see, who took me through the Center, and through the naval base at Le Havre.'' She sipped again, lingering over it. Deboque would already know about her tête-à-tête with Bennett at the museum. So, she would use his knowledge and twist the truth.

"It was a simple matter to ask questions and express interest in how the museum guards its treasures. With that, I was shown the setup, alarms, monitors, sensors." She paused again to let it sink in. "The more a woman pretends ignorance, the more she learns."

Deboque warmed the brandy in his hands. "Hypothetically, you understand, can the security at the palace be broken?"

At last, she thought, they were homing in. "Hypothetically, any security can be broken. I will say that Reeve MacGee has designed an admirable system, but not an invincible one."

"Interesting." He picked up a small china figure of a hawk and began to study it. The room fell into silence long enough for her to be sure he was trying to unnerve her. "And do you have a theory on how this system can be undermined?"

"From inside." She sipped her brandy again. "It's always cleaner from the inside."

"And the Center?"

"Much the same."

"This play the princess wrote, it opens in a few days. It would be amusing to cause a small disturbance."

"Of what nature?"

He only smiled. "Oh, I'm just speaking in theory, you understand. It seems to me that the Royal Family would be uncomfortable if something disrupted the evening. I should hate to miss it. You'll be there?"

"I'm expected." She needed to push him, push him into something definite. "I prefer knowing which door to walk into, *monsieur*."

"Then you might be wise to remain in the audience. I wouldn't want to lose you now that we've become close."

She acknowledged this, but realizing he would demand the rest of the stats then dismiss her, Hannah changed gears. "As a matter of personal curiosity may I ask why you have such interest in the Royal Family? It intrigues me because I see you much as I see myself, as a person most interested in profit and personal gain."

"Profit is always desirable." He set the hawk down. He had hands that might have played a violin or written sonnets. They rarely killed, only gestured for others to do so. "Personal gain can have a multitude of variables, *n'est-ce pas?*"

"As long as it satisfies," she agreed. "Using the kidnapping of the Princess Gabriella or the threats on the Bissets as a lever to gain your release from prison was one thing. You're no longer in prison." Again she looked with admiration around the room. "I would think you would move on to more profitable waters."

"All business needs a completion." She saw emotion for the first time as his fingers tightened around his glass. "All debts require payment. The interest of ten years is dear, very dear. Do you agree?"

"Yes. Revenge, or retribution if you prefer. This I understand is as sweet as diamonds." And looking at him, she knew he would stop at nothing to collect. "*Monsieur*, you have arranged for me to be in the palace. I intend to continue to remain there until you alter the order, but I prefer to do so with some direction." She gestured casually, palm up. "The revenge, after all, is yours, not mine. I've never worked well blindfolded."

"A man who puts all of his cards on the table loses his edge."

"Agreed. So does a man who doesn't sharpen his tools and use them where they're best suited. I'm in, *monsieur*. Having a map of some sort would be useful."

He intended to use her, and well. Sitting back again, Deboque steepled his hands. His diamonds shot out violent light. He had failed, twice before he had failed to use the Bissets for his own purposes. He had failed to bring Armand to his knees. Whatever had to be done, whomever had to be used, he wouldn't fail this time. In Hannah, he thought he'd found the instrument.

"Let me ask you this. If one man wishes to destroy another, what does he do?"

"The simplest is to end his life."

Deboque smiled, and now Hannah saw the evil. It was coated with class, pampered with elegance, but very real. "I'm not a simple man. Death is so final, and even when it is slow, it's soon over. To destroy a man, the soul, the heart, requires more than a bullet in the brain."

He was speaking of Armand, she knew. It wasn't time to demand he name names and reveal his plan. He would tell her nothing and trust her less. Hannah set down her glass and tried to think as he did. "To truly destroy, you take away what is most valuable." Her heart began to beat in the back of her throat, clogging a wave of nausea. Still, when she spoke it was with cool admiration. "His children?"

"You are intelligent as well as lovely." Leaning over he placed his hand on hers. She felt it from him, the vile, dark movement of death. "To make a man suffer, to destroy his soul, you deprive him of what he loves best and leave him to live with it. His children and grandchildren dead, his country in chaos, a man would have nothing left but misery. And a country without an heir becomes unstable—and profitable—if one is shrewd."

"All of them," Hannah murmured. She thought of little Marissa, so pretty and soft, and Dorian with his smudged face and bright grin. Fear for them was suddenly so strong, so vital, she thought it had to show in her eyes. She kept them down, looking at his hand as it lay over hers and the cold, hard glint of the diamonds.

"All of them, *monsieur*?" When she thought she could trust herself again, she looked back at his face. He was smiling. In the fragile light of the chandeliers he looked wan as a ghost and infinitely more frightening. "Not an easy task, even for someone of your power."

"Nothing worthwhile is simple, my dear. But as you said, nothing is impossible—particularly when one is trusted and close."

Her brow lifted. She didn't shudder or draw away. Business, she told herself. Lady Hannah was all business. She was being offered a job, the most vital one Deboque had to offer.

"You were carefully chosen, Lady Hannah. For more than ten years, I've had one dream. I believe you are the instrument to see it to fruition."

She pursed her lips as if considering while her mind raced ahead. He was giving her a contract, a royal one. As she said nothing, his fingers played lightly over her knuckles. Like a spider, she thought, a handsome and very clever spider.

"Such a responsibility is weighty for someone in my position in your organization."

"That can be seen to. Bouffe is—retiring," he said softly. "I will be looking for a replacement."

She let her hand lie under his as she touched her tongue to her top lip. "A guarantee, *monsieur*."

"My word."

She smiled a little. *"Monsieur."*

With a nod of acknowledgement, he rose and pressed a button on his desk. Within seconds Ricardo appeared. "Lady Hannah will be replacing Bouffe. See to the arrangements, Ricardo. Discreetly."

"Of course." The pale green eyes half closed as if with pleasure.

Hannah waited for the door to shut again. A man's life was over. "The day may come when you decide to replace me as casually."

"Not if you continue to please me." He lifted her hand again and kissed it. "I have a feeling you will."

"I must tell you, *monsieur*, I have a distaste for killing children." His fingers tightened, very slightly on hers, but she didn't fidget. "I believe it will take five million American dollars to overcome this distaste."

She saw it in his eyes. He would break her fingers as easily as he would kiss them. Hannah kept her gaze steady on his and hoped she hadn't pushed her luck too far.

"Is it money that seduces you, *ma petite*?"

"Not seduces, pleases. I like to be pleased."

"You have two weeks to please me, Lady Hannah. Then I shall return the favor." He kept her hand in his as he drew her to her feet. "Now, as a show of faith, you will tell me what you failed to note down here."

Hannah walked over to the specs and prepared to lie to him.

She was exhausted. In a decade of assignments, nothing had left her feeling so empty and soiled. As she drove through the palace gates, she could only think about a long hot shower where she could scrub off whatever traces remained of Deboque's cologne. Reeve was standing a hundred feet beyond the gates. Hannah stopped the car and waited for him to slide in beside her.

"You were gone a long time." He gave her a long, thorough study. "It wasn't in the plans for you to be out of contact for over an hour."

"It was in the plans for me to get to Deboque."

"And you did?"

She rolled down her window a bit farther. "I met him on a yacht, the *Invincible*. It's anchored about five miles northwest. He has at least six armed guards, double that by a guess. He has the information we wanted him to have. I'm replacing Bouffe."

Reeve's brow lifted. "You must have impressed him."

"That was the idea." She wondered how soon she could wash the taste of his brandy from her mouth. "He's planning something for the opening of Eve's play." When Reeve stiffened beside her, she went on. "I don't believe it's going to be anything directly against the family. He seemed to think it would be entertaining to confuse matters. He's very careful how he phrases things. Nothing too direct. Even if I testified against him, it would be difficult to actually convict him of conspiracy. He hypothesizes, theorizes."

"Did he give you an idea where he intends to make his move?"

She listened for a moment to a bird that was singing its heart out. "He seemed most interested in the palace. It's the biggest challenge. We have two weeks."

"He moves in two weeks?"

"That's how long he gave me to murder your family." She turned to him then and saw his face was pale and set. "All of you but Armand, Reeve. The children, everyone. He wants to destroy Armand's soul and leave Cordina without an heir. If you trust my judgment, he wants this done as much for personal satisfaction as for the profit he might make when Cordina is thrown into chaos."

Reeve drew out a cigarette but didn't light it. "I trust your judgment."

"We have two weeks to stop him, or to convince him that I've done what he wants."

It was his family, his heart, yet he knew he had to think as coolly as she did. "Is he setting you up?"

She thought for a moment, then shook her head. "I don't think so. It's certainly possible that he'd dispose of me after I've finished the job, but I think it's more likely he'd continue to use me. We did a good job of planting information about me, and over the past two years I've saved him a bit of trouble and money. If he believes I can give him this, he'll sit back and wait."

"Armand will have to be told."

"I know." But not Bennett. Armand and only Armand.

"For now, just go on as usual." He indicated that she should drive ahead. "We'll need some time."

"Eve's opening is in a few days."

"We'll handle it. You get some sleep. As soon as we have a direction, I'll let you know."

Hannah got out of the car, then as Reeve stood on the other side she stopped. "I want him. I want him for myself. I know it's unprofessional and stupid. But if I have the chance, if I find the way, I'm going to take him out myself."

Reeve said nothing as she walked up the steps. He'd already vowed the same thing.

Chapter Eight

"I don't want you to go tonight."

"You know I have to." Eve stood, grim and stubborn, facing her husband. "It's my play, my troupe, my production. I don't have a choice, Alex."

"Excuses can be made." He looked at her, dressed in midnight blue that skimmed her shoulders and swirled to her ankles. Her hair was caught up in the back so that it fell over one shoulder like ebony. Even after all the years he'd known her, just looking at her made his pulse race. "You know how dangerous it could be. With the information we have now, we can be sure there'll be an incident tonight. I don't want you involved."

"I am involved." She was frightened. Ever since Reeve had told them that he'd received a tip that there would be trouble at the theater on opening night, her nerves had been stretched tight. Yes, she was frightened, but she was no less determined. She crossed to the beveled mirror above the bureau as if checking the arrangement of her hair was of some importance. "I wrote the play, I produced it, and more important than either of those," she continued before he could interrupt, "I belong at the theater tonight because I'm your wife."

The fact that her arguments were valid meant nothing. He wanted her in the palace, safe, untouchable. His heart would rest easy if he knew she was here, in the suite of rooms she'd decorated, tucked high in the palace that had been his family home for generations. Nothing could happen to her here. Anything could happen outside.

"My love, Reeve is rarely wrong. If he says there'll be trouble tonight, I want you well away from it. The fact that you're carrying a child is a very simple reason for you to be excused. I know the play is important to you, but—"

"Yes, it is," she interrupted. "But you're more important."

"Then do this for me, and stay home tonight."

She tilted her head, holding on to both her nerves and her temper. "Alexander, would you stay behind with me?"

"If it was possible, of course." Impatience had him dragging a hand through his hair. It was a ploy she'd used before, and one there was little argument against. "I can't close myself up every time there's a rumble from Deboque."

"For Cordina," she said quietly. "And Cordina is now my country, too."

"Eve." He thought he loved her as much as it was possible to love. Every day he learned there could be more. "You are the most precious thing in the world to me. I almost lost you once."

She crossed to him then, knowing the first step, the first touch should be hers. When both of his hands were in hers, she looked up into his eyes. "And I you, Alex. I'm going to sit in the Royal Box beside you, where I belong."

From outside the door, Hannah heard the conversation clearly enough. It was moments like this that made it difficult to think of what she was doing, what she had yet to do, as merely another assignment. There were people beyond the door whom she'd come to care about. The Bissets were no longer names or symbols, but friends. After ten years of playing dangerous games, she knew how risky it could be to make friends.

She closed her eyes and drew her breath deep before she knocked.

"Entrez." It was Alexander who answered, the impatience in his voice ripe. Hannah opened the door but didn't cross the threshold.

"I'm sorry. I'm disturbing you."

"Of course not." With the warmth that was so much a part of her, Eve smiled and gestured her inside. "I see you're ready for the evening." She felt a little twinge of regret at Hannah's severe beige dress and hairstyle. She'd hoped with a little time she could urge Hannah to soften her image. Tonight, however, there were more immediate matters of concern. "We were just about to come down ourselves."

Hannah saw Eve take Alexander's hand again. "I thought you might need some help."

"No, there's nothing." But the cloud of concern didn't leave Eve's eyes. "Hannah, I don't want you to feel obligated to go with the family. Knowing there's a possibility of an—incident," she began. "Well, it might be more comfortable for you here at home."

"Of course I'm going." With the hated secret tucked inside of her, she shifted the wrap on her arms. "And I really believe everything's going to be fine. If you don't need me then, I'll just go down."

"Please, let's not talk about it anymore," Eve said when Hannah shut the door behind her. "Let's go say good-night to Marissa before we leave."

"Eve." Alexander gathered her close. He could feel the slight swell where another child lay. "I love you."

"Talk's cheap," she murmured, and tried for a laugh. "Promise to show me later, after the play."

He let his cheek rest on her hair. "You have my word."

Bennett was already waiting in the main hall. Even with the distance separating them, Hannah could feel the impatience coming from him. Impatience, she thought, mixed with a recklessness that the elegant evening clothes couldn't disguise. He was looking for trouble, Hannah realized. More, he was hoping for it.

"There you are." Though he smiled up at her, his mind was already on the evening ahead. Instinctively he took her hand, holding it as she reached the bottom of the stairs. "You don't have to go tonight, Hannah. I'd be happier if you didn't."

Guilt came so quickly that she had squeezed his hand in reassurance before she could stop herself. "Now even you sound like Eve," she said lightly. "I want to be there. A vague tip from an anonymous source is a foolish reason to miss a night at the theater."

He touched the pearl cluster at her ear. "Is that what we call British pluck?"

"It's what we call common sense."

"Whatever it's called I want you to stay close. There'll be enough guards to smother us, but I prefer to keep an eye on you myself." Before she could stop him, he was leading her toward the doors.

"Eve and Alexander are nearly ready. I said I'd wait for them."

"Security feels better splitting us up." He acknowledged Claude with a brief nod. "You'll ride with me. Father will come along after Alexander and Eve."

"All right." She walked out into the star-studded night, calmly holding the .22 that lay within her beaded evening bag.

The theater was sold out. Long before the first curtain, the seats were filled so that the babble of conversation rose up to the Royal Box. There was thunderous applause when the Bissets entered. From the background as bows were made, Hannah held her breath and studied the sea of faces.

If Deboque had been there, she knew she would have found him.

"The Center's been swept twice," Reeve murmured in her ear. "There's nothing here."

She nodded and took her seat as the curtain rose.

The play was everything Eve had hoped for, though Hannah doubted anyone in the box had their full attention on the drama and pathos onstage. More than once, she cast a sidelong look at Bennett to find him studying the audience.

Deboque wasn't there. Hannah hadn't expected him. Whatever happened, whenever it happened, he would be far away with an alibi as solid as Cordinian rock.

So they would wait. And watch.

When the lights came up for intermission, Hannah could almost feel Eve relax. A false alarm? No. Though she preferred that Eve believe it was so, Hannah knew better. There was an itch between her shoulder blades, vague but persistent. Some called it a hunch. Others called it instinct. Hannah had been in the game long enough to know when to wait and when to go with it.

"Would you like something to drink?"

She turned to Bennett, set to refuse. For personal reasons, she wanted him close at hand. "Yes," she heard herself saying, knowing this would be just one more deception. "I'd love something cool."

The moment he was through the doors behind them, Hannah leaned toward Reeve. "I'm going to look around."

"I'd stay close—I have a feeling." With him it was in the gut. He'd yet to let Gabriella move more than an arm's span away.

"I do too. Deboque said something about me staying in the audience. I want to take a walk backstage."

He started to object, but Gabriella took his hand and gave Hannah the few seconds she needed to slip out. She made her way toward the ladies' lounge until she was certain no one was watching. With the ease of long experience, she slipped into a stairway and began moving down. She had ten minutes, Hannah thought as she checked her watch, before anyone would miss her.

There were costume changes and stretched nerves backstage when Hannah crossed the corridor. Most of the actors were too wound up to spare her a glance. Nothing out of place. Nothing out of synch. And yet, the itch between her shoulder blades persisted.

Chantel's dressing room door was half-open. The actress caught a glimpse of Hannah, hesitated, then called out. "Lady Hannah."

Because she saw no choice, Hannah stopped at the doorway. "Miss O'Hurley. Her Highness wasn't able to come down, but you should know she's delighted with your performance."

"Thank you." Chantel set down the grease pencil she'd been using to touch up her eyes. "And what do you think of the play?"

"It's gripping. Your interpretation of Julia is breathtaking."

With a nod, Chantel moved toward her. The exaggerated stage makeup only made her look more exotic. "You know, I was born into show business. It's in the blood, if you get my drift. And I've always thought one inveterate actor easily recognizes another."

Very cool, almost smiling, Hannah met her eyes. "I suppose that's true."

"Perhaps that's why while I'm still not sure if I like you, I know I don't trust you." Chantel adjusted the cuff of the dress she'd wear in the next scene. "I've always been very fond of Bennett. A woman like myself has few men she can call real friends."

There was something strong, something honest in the woman who faced her. Hannah gave as much as she could. "I can tell you that Bennett is a special man, and one I care for very much."

Chantel was silent a moment, weighing, considering. "I'm not sure why, but I believe you." She shook her head. "I can't figure out why you're playing Jane Eyre, but I imagine you have your reasons."

"Places, Miss O'Hurley."

Chantel turned to give herself one last check in a full-length mirror. She lifted her chin to a different angle and became Julia. Her voice took on the slightest of drawls, an echo of the American South, as she turned back to walk past Hannah. "Darling," she said in character. "You must know beige is the worst possible color for you." Then she winked and walked to the wings.

Hannah let out a long breath. She'd seen nothing out of place, seen no one who didn't belong and had learned a lesson. Her cover wasn't as foolproof as she'd always thought.

She walked back down the corridor, turned into the stairway and started up. She heard the applause as the curtain came up. Then came the distant sound, the rumble and boom, of an explosion. The lights went out.

There were scattered screams as the theater plunged into darkness. From here, the warning rumble couldn't be heard. In the Royal Box, guards closed in like a wedge. Guns were drawn and held ready.

"Stay where you are," Reeve ordered. He gave Gabriella's hand a quick, reassuring squeeze. "Two of you come with me." He moved into the hallway with two guards. "We'll need a light." Swearing, he dug in his pocket for a lighter. "We'll need someone to go over the PA and keep the audience from panicking." Even as he flicked the lighter on, throwing dull and shadowy light off his face, Chantel's voice came cool and clear through the speakers.

"*Mesdames and messieurs*, if you would stay seated for a moment or two. We seem to be having some difficulties with the lights. If you'd like to take advantage of the opportunity by getting to know your neighbor better..."

"Good girl," Reeve murmured as he heard the nervous laughter. "Let's get down to the main breakers."

Hannah hadn't come back. The words kept echoing over in Bennett's mind as he heard Alexander murmuring reassurances to Eve. She was out there somewhere, alone in the dark. Without hesitation, he was moving toward the door.

"Your Highness." The looming figure of a guard inched toward him. "If you would please remain seated."

"Let me pass."

"Bennett." His father's voice cut through the dark. "Please sit. This should be over in moments."

"Hannah's not here."

There was the briefest of silences. "Reeve will handle things."

There was duty, and the honor he'd never questioned. Now there was love. Bennett shoved his way through the door and went to find her.

Hannah had the gun in her hand as she stood in the stairwell. She didn't move, barely breathed, as she debated whether to go up and check on the Bissets, or whether to go down and check the power. If there had been one bomb, there could all too easily be another.

Her head told her that the Bissets were well guarded and her job was to find the source of the trouble. Her heart wanted only to see if Bennett was well and safe. Following it, Hannah started up the stairs. She'd climbed no more than three when she heard the sound of a door closing on the landing below.

With her finger wrapped around the trigger, she pointed the barrel of the gun up and started down again. She saw the beam of the flashlight before she heard the footsteps. Cautious ones. Quiet ones. Like a shadow, Hannah melted into a corner and waited.

She recognized him from the museum. He was dressed now in the dark blue uniform of the maintenance crew and carried a small toolbox. She almost nodded in approval. Anyone seeing him would simply assume he was assigned to fix whatever had gone wrong. The beam skimmed passed the toes of her shoes before she stepped out and pressed the gun at his side.

"Be easy," she said in undertones. "I apologize for greeting you this way, but I didn't want a hole in my head before you recognized me."

"*Mademoiselle.*" She heard the tightly controlled fury in his voice. No man liked to be caught unaware. "I was told you would remain out of the way this evening."

Hannah drew the gun back but kept it steady. "I prefer a firsthand look at what's going on. A dramatic distraction," she complimented him. "Are there other plans for tonight?" He was prepared to kill, she was certain. But was he armed? She knew if she detained him too long or pressed too hard, her cover would be in jeopardy.

"Only if the opportunity arises. You will excuse me?"

"Certainly." Her only thought now was to see him out of the theater and away before any opportunity arose. The theater was packed with people, the Royal Family was present. Now wasn't the time for a confrontation. "Can I assist you in making a discreet exit?"

"It's been seen to."

"Very well. Tell our employer that I won't be as dramatic, but I'll be effective." She turned toward the stairs when she heard the door above open.

"Hannah?"

At the sound of Bennett's voice her blood froze. Even as the man beside her made a move, she clamped a hand over is arm. She knew without seeing that he reached for a weapon.

"Don't be a fool," she hissed. "In this light you could too easily miss and ruin everything. Turn off that beam and let me handle it." She felt his resistance, but turned quickly and started up the stairs. "Bennett." She didn't have to fake the fear in her voice. He was hardly more than a shadow at the doorway but she put her arms around him and let her body lock his.

"What are you doing down here?" he began.

"I lost my way when the lights went off."

"For God's sake, Hannah. How did you manage to get all the way down here?"

"I—I'm not sure. Please, let's go back."

"You could've broken your neck on these stairs." When he gave her a slight shake and started to draw her back she shifted to block him more thoroughly.

"Kiss me," she ordered in a whisper.

Almost amused now that he'd found her safe, Bennett lifted up her chin. In the dim light he could only make out the vague outline of her face and the glint of her eyes. "If you insist."

Even as he closed his mouth over hers, she gripped the door handle behind him, prepared to shove him through.

Then his fingers spread over her face, gently. His lips coaxed and comforted and asked so little in return. On the handle her fingers tightened as much in response to him as fear for him. One hand settled at the small of her back, again to soothe. Hannah felt her heart tear. She loved him, yet knew she couldn't. She wanted the kiss to be no more than what it was, a merging of lips, a symbol of caring. But what it was, what it had to be was a tool to give the man below them the time to escape.

Then Bennett would be safe. For seconds only, she put her heart into the kiss. He would be safe, and she could breathe again.

He felt the change and his heart thudded with it. He had imagined her lost in the dark, alone and in need of comfort and physical contact. So thinking, he had buried his own needs and had kissed her as a friend might, with affection and understanding. Her response was thunder and lightning. His fingers tightened on her face as he murmured her name.

The lights came on in a flash.

It happened very quickly then, but Bennett would remember, for a lifetime, each movement, each sound. There was no time for fear, only for surprise, then disillusionment.

When the lights went on, he stiffened. She knew in that moment that Deboque's man had not made his escape as she had hoped, but was waiting to take advantage of the opportunity that had presented itself. Without hesitation she whirled out of Bennett's arms and half shoved him through the door. The man's gun was drawn, but so was hers. And she was very fast.

Bennett had seen the man, and his weapon. He had pushed himself off the door to shield her even as she'd fired. For a moment, he simply stared, stunned at seeing the man fall and lie still. Then he saw the pistol in Hannah's hand. Surprise came and went. His face became very impassive. When he spoke, his voice was neutral.

"What game are you playing, and for whom?"

She'd never killed before. She'd been trained to, of course, but had never actually ended a life by her own hand. As she stood looking down, the gun felt foreign and slim in her hand. Her face was very pale, her eyes very dark when she turned to Bennett. "I'll have to explain, but there isn'

ime." She heard the sound of running feet and struggled to
ull herself together. "Please trust me."

"That's an interesting request at this point." He started
o brush by her to go to the man below.

"Bennett, please." Grabbing his arm, she drew up be-
ide him. "I'll tell you whatever I can later. You can verify
t all with Reeve or your father."

She felt his muscles tense. "My father?"

"Please, for his sake, the sake of your family, play this
ut with me." She pushed the gun into his hand just as
Reeve arrived with five guards on his heels. Now she let re-
ction set it. Again, truth was often the best cover.

"He tried to shoot the prince." Hannah let her voice
hake and leaned heavily against Bennett. "He was going to
ill him. If Bennett hadn't..." Trailing off, she buried her
ace against Bennett's shoulder.

He didn't move, though he didn't contradict her, there
vas no comforting hand now, no murmured reassurances.
Reeve bent over the body, then lifted his gaze and met Ben-
ett's. "It's fortunate you were quick—and accurate." The
45 lying beside the body hadn't been fired. His eyes shifted
ver briefly to rest on Hannah. "We'll handle this quietly."

Bennett's lips curved, but it wasn't a smile. "Of course."

"If you'll go back to your box." Reeve signaled two of
he guards to accompany him. "We'll say nothing of this to
he family until we can be private." With a pencil, he lifted
he .45 automatic by the trigger guard. "The police will
ome in the back way."

Bennett brushed the guards aside with a gesture. It was
he first time Hannah had seen him use true royal arro-
ance. "I want to talk to you. Alone. Now."

"All right." He'd seen too much, Reeve knew. It had to
e handled quickly. "Eve's office then. If you'd give me a
ew minutes to deal with this first."

"You have ten," Bennett said, and turned his back on all of them.

"I'd like to go back to the palace." Hannah stood on the steps, alone now. Her hands, white at the knuckles, clutched her bag. "I'm not feeling well."

"See to a car and driver," Reeve ordered one of the guards. To another he gave the dead man's weapon before he climbed the stairs to slip an arm around Hannah. "I'll walk you out." The moment they were out of earshot, his voice became curt and professional. "What happened?"

Her knees were shaking, but she schooled her voice to the same tone. Briefly, she gave him her report. "The entire thing couldn't have taken more than five minutes." It had seemed like hours.

"It was just bad luck all around that Bennett found you. Still, the story will hold. He has a reputation for being an excellent shot. All I have to do is calm him down." Reeve let out a long breath at that. He knew his brother-in-law well, just as he knew all the Bissets. Once their temper was lost, it wasn't easily regained. "We'll go over this in the morning, so that the story you pass on to Deboque is the most advantageous one."

"He'll never forgive me."

Reeve was intuitive enough to know she wasn't speaking of Deboque now. "Bennett is neither unjust nor hardhearted. He'll be angry at being kept in the dark, but he won't blame you."

"Won't he?" Hannah walked through the doors and into the night air without looking back.

She sat by the window looking out at the garden. An hour had passed, then two while she watched the moonlight. The palace was quiet. Perhaps the others had come back, but she wouldn't have heard because her rooms faced the back.

Guests were always given the loveliest views and the quietest spots.

She could imagine all too well how Bennett would have reacted to Reeve's explanations. But it wouldn't be Reeve he would blame. Hannah knew the blame would be hers and had accepted it. In the morning he would probably demand to speak with her privately.

She wouldn't apologize. Hannah lifted her chin a fraction higher. She would accept his anger and his coldness, but she wouldn't apologize for being who and what she was.

She loved him. He would hardly believe her now if she had the right to tell him. She would have died for him tonight, not only for duty, not only for honor, but so much more for love. He would never understand or believe that now. Perhaps it was best. If her feelings for him had gotten beyond her control, it was wiser, and safer, if his for her had deadened.

She still had an assignment to complete and two years of work to finish.

Hannah laid her head on the windowsill and wished she were in London where the night would be cold and damp and smell of the river.

He didn't knock. The time for manners, formalities and small kindnesses had passed. She was curled on the window seat with her arms folded on the sill and her head resting on them. She'd loosened her hair so that it fell over the shoulders and down the back of a plain white robe. A man could almost believe she was a woman lost in the night. Bennett no longer believed what he saw and little that he felt. When he shut the door behind him, she was up and standing quickly.

She hadn't expected him that night. Looking at his face, Hannah saw that she should have. Because she knew the worst when she faced it, she braced.

"You spoke with Reeve?"

"Yes."

"And your father?"

His brow lifted. Though he had discarded his formal jacket, he could be very much the prince when he chose. "We talk tomorrow, though that doesn't concern you."

She acknowledged this with a slight nod. "Only inasmuch as it affects my position at the moment."

"Although you're obviously unaware of it, I'm not a fool. Your position remains." He took the small pistol from his pocket. After crossing to the stand beside her bed, he set it down. "Your property."

No, she would not be forgiven. She'd thought she'd been ready to accept it. She'd been wrong. "Thank you." As coolly as he, she walked to the stand, then placed the pistol in the drawer.

"You're an excellent shot, Lady Hannah."

The drawer shut again with the slightest of slams. "I've been well trained."

He caught her chin then, not gently. "Yes, by God, you have. What other talents do you have, I wonder? Deceit is certainly the sharpest. How many women can you be?

"However many it takes to do my job. If you'd excuse me, I'm very tired."

"Oh, no." With his other hand, he gathered up her hair. He thought of what she'd put him through in one evening. Anxiety, outright terror and betrayal. "I'm afraid I won't fall for that again. With me, at any rate, the quiet, well-bred English lady is quite done. Cards on the table, Hannah."

It was fear, she realized, that had her stomach heaving. Not fear that he would hurt her physically, not fear that he would do something in temper that would jeopardize the operation, but fear, deadly and cold, that he would always look at her the way he was now.

"I doubt there's much I can tell you that Reeve hasn't. The operation was put in effect just over two years ago. The ISS needed an agent on the inside, so—"

"I've been apprised of the basic details." He let her go, dropping his hands to his sides. There, they balled into fists. "A bit late, but the information seems fairly complete. After establishing yourself with Deboque's organization, you pretended an affection for Eve so you could gain access to the palace." He saw the flicker of emotion cross her face at that but wasn't ready to interpret it. "In this way, Deboque would be deceived into believing he had one of his own on the inside. By playing both ends, you would be privy to his plans, and once he makes a move, the authorities would be able to close in and destroy his organization. I'm told I should be grateful you're so good at what you do."

"I don't need gratitude, just cooperation."

"Then perhaps you should have asked for it from the beginning."

She lifted her head. No, there would be no apologies. "I had orders, Bennett. You're no stranger to duty."

"No, but neither am I a stranger to honor. You played me." Anger broke through the ice so that he held both of her arms. "You used my feelings for you."

"You weren't supposed to have any," she snapped back.

"We can't always choose what we feel. But there are other choices. Did you need to use how I felt for you, Hannah?"

"I had a job to do." Her voice wasn't steady now because she couldn't be sure if she'd done what she'd done coolly or because of her own needs. "I tried to discourage you."

"You knew I cared, that I wanted you."

"I didn't want you to."

"You still lie."

"No." She yanked, but he held her firm. "I did nothing to attract you. Then again, perhaps a woman only has to exist for you to be attracted." She saw the fury bloom but ignored it. "Perhaps by refusing to sleep with you, I became more of a challenge. There are a lot of women who would gladly sleep with royalty."

"Do you believe if all I had wanted was you in bed that you wouldn't have been there a half-a-dozen times already?"

"I go nowhere I don't take myself." She tossed her head back. His voice had been too low, too precise, but she was past caring. "If you're angry because I'm not what you thought I was, it's because your ego's been bruised."

The rest of her words and her breath were knocked away as she fell under him on the bed. Before she could counter the move, her arms were pinned at her sides. She'd been warned about his temper. There had even been some documentation of it in his dossier. But none of that was nearly as awesome as seeing it first hand.

"Ego?" He gritted out with his face only inches from hers. "So to you I'm still only what you've read, only what you've been told." It hurt, how it hurt. He could feel it shimmer inside of him until the only recourse was to turn it into anger. "I won't disappoint you then."

She scissored her legs and nearly succeeded in rocking him off. He shifted until her body was pressed flat against his. One hand rested dangerously on her throat. It gave him grim pleasure to feel her pulse flutter rapidly beneath his fingers.

"This won't prove anything." She managed to free one arm, but he caught it at the wrist. Her pulse beat there as well, fast, uneven. "You'll only demean both of us."

It didn't matter. He'd gone beyond right and wrong, truth and lies. "There was a time when I believed you to be shy and precious. That was a woman I only wanted to show tenderness to. For her I had such patience, such sweet feelings. But for you, we can dispense with such things, can't we?"

"Bennett, don't do this." She said it quietly, knowing it was already too late.

"Why not?" The recklessness was back, in full force, driven by betrayal. "It's a night for lies and passions."

She prepared to do battle, for herself and for him. "You won't rape me."

"No, I won't. But I will have you."

Chapter Nine

It would be a battle of wits, a contest for control. Somehow it was easier for Hannah to think of that when Bennett's lips pressed down on hers. He didn't want to make love with her, but to punish, even to conquer. It was anger, not desire that had brought them here. She couldn't afford to forget it, not even for an instant.

Yet the kiss wasn't cruel. Hot and hard he moved his mouth over hers, more taunting than insistent. The hand on her throat didn't so much threaten as control. The callused fingers reminded her of the strength in his hands even as they stroked to arouse and seduce.

She made her body lie still and limp beneath his, waiting not just for a chance to fight back, but for a chance to fight and win.

But her blood was already beginning to stir.

He knew it. He was a man who understood passions, desires, vulnerabilities and how one would feed on the others. He'd used such things before, all in good humor, to give as much as to take. Now he would use them to wound as deeply as he had been wounded.

Women had frustrated him, amused him, baffled him and fascinated him. But no woman had ever hurt him before Hannah. That she'd done so not inadvertently, not in a fit of temper, but coolly, passionlessly, made the sin unforgivable. For the first time in his life he held a woman in his arms with the sole intention of bringing her pain.

Or so he told himself.

There was only flesh beneath the robe. He knew it before he drew the material down her bare shoulder. There was strength there. He'd felt it once before. Now he felt the softness as well. Both moved him, just as, he discovered, his touch moved her. As she began her first struggles, he shifted so that her loosened robe parted for him.

She knew better than to panic, but her heart and her needs betrayed her. The moment he'd stroked his palm down her bare skin the flare of pleasure had opened the door to fear. To excitement. To passion. Her struggles took them rolling over the bed, locked in combat. His lean build and easygoing manner made the steely strength she discovered both a surprise and an arousal. Muscles bunched under his shirt as he countered her moves and took her where he wanted her to go. Hannah found herself trapped beneath him again with her arms pinned by the robe that had slipped down her back.

Breathless, she stared up at him. She was beaten, but far from ready to submit. Moonlight slanted in over her face so that her skin was milky pale, her eyes dark and glowing. The fear in them had turned to condemnation. In a mass of confusion, her hair spread over the bed, making him think of mermaids and witches.

"I'll despise you."

Something ripped quietly inside him. His heart or perhaps his soul. He ignored it and fixed on the need to punish her for making him love an illusion.

He lowered his mouth again, but she turned her head away. A small defense, and an unwise one as his lips found the soft, vulnerable curve of her throat. Her breath caught, then expelled again on a moan. The sound had his heart drumming as he found her taste as unique and as dangerous as his feelings for her.

He wanted to love her, and to hate her. He needed to comfort and to punish. He sought to hurt and to give pleasure. In the midst of his confusion, he forgot everything but Hannah.

Hardened from work, gentle by nature, his hands moved over her. With the tip of his tongue, he traced patterns, tormenting, tempting patterns over her skin. He could feel it heat beneath him so that the flavor and the softness seemed to intensify. She twisted one way under him, then the other so that her agitated movements only served to arouse them both.

All at once her body became very still, almost as if even breathing had stopped. Then the trembling began.

She'd never been more aware of herself, more distanced from rational thought. She wanted to remember why he was with her, why it was wrong for both of them, but could only feel. Reasons no longer mattered, consequences were forgotten. He wanted. She wanted. Right and wrong were for the sane.

When he brought his mouth back to hers again, she was waiting. He didn't find pliancy or panic, but the passion she had ruthlessly strapped down most of her life. For him it was free, and she had a fleeting moment to realize it would never fully be disguised again.

Impatience. Desperation. Together they rolled over the bed again but in a far different kind of combat. Her robe was lost so that her arms were free to capture him. In a move that might have told him everything, she locked him to her.

Stay with me. Love me. Understand me.

Then even that was lost in a torrent of heat that left them both gasping.

Once before he'd sensed a volcano inside of her. Now as it erupted around him, he was rocked by the power, the dark violence of it. The breeze that fluttered the curtains was cool and temperate. In the center of the bed was a furnace each of them stoked higher and higher.

Frantic for more of him, Hannah pulled his shirt open, scattering buttons over the mattress and floor. When her laugh came, it was low and sultry as he'd heard it before, but now it had an edge of something that might have been triumph. Then it was a sigh as she ran her hands up his chest. Her kiss was hot and hungry on his as naked flesh met naked flesh.

Something snapped inside him. As a lover he'd always been clever, considerate, caring. Love had never been a game to him, nor had it been a contest. Always, it had been a result of affection, a natural culmination of needs.

But he'd never needed like this.

Tenderness was forgotten as completely as revenge as he dove his hands into her hair and dragged her against him. His teeth nipped into her lower lip, sending dizzying sparks of pleasure through her. Then he began to move swiftly, leaving her lips unsatisfied while his kisses tortured and tamed wherever they reached.

There was panic again, but so twined with excitement she could recognize neither. Afraid, aroused, she tried to draw him back when with a suddenness that left her gasping, he drove her up and over. Her body contracted, almost in defense, then filled with a rush of heat that had her blood burning. Release came on a flood, on a cry of his name, and with the knowledge that no one would ever take her there but him.

She was weak and shuddering. The hands that had clutched the bed clothes went lax. For a moment, she began to float. Then he fanned the flames again.

This is what he'd wanted for her, from her. Her skin was damp and soft under his hands. Her muscles were limber as he began to move with him again. In the moonlight, he saw her face, dazed with passion, flushed with pleasure. Cupping her hips in his hands, he started a lingering line of kisses up her body. He could feel the moment the strength poured back into her.

Still shuddering, still breathless, she tugged at his slacks. She'd had a sample, a taste, and wanted more. She wanted all. As she pulled his clothes from him, he skimmed his fingertips over her inner thighs, hampering her progress, arousing her unbearably. He watched her eyes fly open with the shock of the fresh climax as her body arched up and strained toward the power. Then even as her muscles went lax, his mouth was on hers again and urging her along the next journey.

He was a drug. Her arms felt like lead as she tried to lift them for him. Her head was spinning from the flood of sensations. The ripe scent of passion covered both of them so that their skin was slick and hot. She could hear her own breath come in sighs and moans as she struggled to focus on his face.

His eyes were tawny, like a cat's before it springs. She remembered how he'd looked on the stallion, daring, dangerous. She shuddered once, then surrendered. With her eyes open and her heart willing, she gathered him close.

She opened. He filled.

The ride was fast and rough. Locked together, they raced. Without slackening pace, they plunged headlong over the cliff.

Silence seemed to last forever. Hannah curled herself into it and waited for him to leave her. Though her mind wasn't cool, some sanity had returned. Covered by the dark, she could admit to herself that she would never be the same. He'd broken through that carefully polished veneer and had conquered the inner woman, the woman he hated. She couldn't tell him that she loved, that she already mourned the loss of what she never really had and would spend the rest of her life wishing for it.

He wanted to reach out to her, to gather her close and stroke her hair in the moonlight. It wouldn't be possible to touch her again. He'd taken in anger what he'd once dreamed of taking in tenderness. The guilt was there, real and ripe even as the sense of betrayal crept back.

The woman he'd fallen in love with didn't exist. She'd been a lie even more than an illusion. Now he'd done what even in his wildest moments he'd avoided. He'd made love with a stranger. And God help him, he'd fallen just as deeply in love with her.

Had he hurt her? He wanted to ask, but held himself back. He couldn't afford to feel remorse or he would end up making a fool of himself over this new Hannah as well. Pride followed honor. Since he'd sacrificed one to temper and pain, he would hold firm to the other.

As he rose, he dragged a hand through his hair. How could he love her when he didn't even know her? How could he still love the woman he knew had never existed.

He dressed in silence while Hannah lay still as a stone on the bed.

"Now it seems we've used each other," he murmured.

She opened her eyes then. There were no tears in them. Thank God she still had the strength for that much. He was standing by the bed, naked from the waist with the ruined shirt balled in his hand. "We can consider ourselves even."

"Can we?" His fingers went white on his shirt. He'd nearly taken a step toward her before he made himself turn and leave her alone.

Hannah lay and listened to the silence until dawn.

"You have questions," Armand began as he faced his youngest son. The morning light was strong through the open windows and showed, all too clearly, the marks of a sleepless night on both faces. "I prefer it if you wait to ask them until after I've finished."

He'd been prepared to demand and to rage. The lines of strain and weariness made his father look suddenly old and much too vulnerable. Again, it was love rather than duty that guided him. "All right." Because he needed it, Bennett poured coffee and left it black.

"Will you sit?"

"No."

Armand's gaze sharpened at the tone. Then he, too, let love hold sway. "I shall." Once seated, he set his untouched coffee aside. "Two years ago, I sat in this office with Reeve and Malori. You and Alexander were also present. You remember?"

Bennett paced to the window and looked out. "Yes. We were speaking of Deboque and what could and should be done."

"Then you remember that Reeve, even then, had an operative in mind to infiltrate the organization."

"I remember, too, that it was decided that the name be kept from Alex and me." The trace of resentment he had felt then had grown to true bitterness in one night. "And that Malori was not completely satisfied with Reeve's choice."

"Malori has always been one of the most trusted members of the security staff in Cordina. But he's old fashioned." Armand saw no need to add that he, too, had had his doubts. "He was concerned with using a woman."

Bennett downed half his coffee. "I felt then, as I feel now, that Alexander and I had a right to know what was being done. More, all of us had the right to know that the woman we accepted as friend was an ISS agent."

"I felt then as I feel now—" Armand's voice, though quiet, held the whip of authority "—that neither of you had a need to know. If I had become ill, Alex, of course, would have been apprised. However—"

"Do you think because I won't rule, Cordina is of less importance to me?" Bennett whirled on his father. The fury

n his face was lethal. "All of my life I've been the younger
rother. Alex was born to rule Cordina after you. He was
molded for it, just as his son will be. Do you think because
f that I cared less, loved less or would have offered less?"

Armand said nothing for a moment, knowing the words
had to be chosen with care, even as they came from the
heart. "Bennett, I've watched you grow from child to man
and have waited for a sign, for a hint that you resented your
position. You have been sometimes wild, always reckless
and too often indiscreet, but never have I seen anything in
ou but love and devotion for your country and your fam-
ly."

"Then why, when something threatens both, do you keep
our plans from me?"

There was a headache drumming behind Armand's tem-
le. He closed his eyes a moment, but didn't lift a hand to
soothe it. "Two years ago, Lady Hannah Rothchild was
chosen out of a half dozen highly qualified operatives to
infiltrate and destroy Deboque's organization. We were
aware, as she was, of the risks involved, and the time and
kill it would take to succeed."

"Why her?" Bennett found he didn't want to think be-
ond that for a moment. It was an answer he had to have
before he could deal with the others.

"Reeve felt Hannah's talents were uniquely suited to the
operation. She's been with the ISS for ten years."

"Ten years?" Bennett roamed the room again as he tried
o take it in. "How is that possible? She's so young."

"She's second generation," Armand said mildly. "Her
father trained her himself while she was still in school. Lord
Rothchild, though semiretired now, is one of the most valued agents in the ISS. He had some part in Reeve's early
raining which was another reason Reeve leaned toward
Hannah for this assignment."

"Ten years," Bennett repeated. How many women had she been? How many lies had she told?

"Apparently she had a natural aptitude for this kind of work." He saw his son's jaw set, but went on. "After reading Reeve's report on her, I had to agree that she was best suited for what we had in mind."

"Deboque often uses women," Bennett murmured.

"He feels they can be more cunning, even more cruel, than men." Armand remembered Janet Smithers and the bullet that had been dug out of his son's flesh. "His preference runs to a certain type, quiet, well-bred, spotless pedigrees."

"Hannah."

"Yes. It was those qualities in her which weighed the decision in her favor. With the cooperation of the ISS a deep background was created for her. The credentials she was given made it possible for her to slip into Deboque's company. In two years, she's moved from messenger to the top of the organization."

"The top?" The fear started then, like something foul in the back of his throat. "What do you mean?"

"She's met with Deboque himself, and by managing to discredit one of his top men, is now filling that position herself. Reeve explained to you that as far as Deboque knows, she's here at the palace as his instrument."

Bitterness was more palatable than fear. He concentrated on it. "She plays the game very well."

"An agent in her position plays the game well or loses her life. You know firsthand that Deboque doesn't hesitate to kill. Her name and the operation itself were kept in strictest confidence not to protect you or the rest of the family, Bennett, but to protect her."

Bennett set his cup down and stopped pacing. "In what way?"

"Three other agents have been killed trying to do what Hannah has nearly succeeded in doing. The last was butchered." He watched Bennett's face pale. He would have spared his son this, as a father. Now, as prince, he could spare him nothing. "By bringing her here in this way, letting you, all of you, believe what Deboque wanted you to believe, Hannah had the only protection we could offer. If she's discovered, even the ISS can't protect her. Now that you know all that you know, her risk is greater than ever."

In silence, Bennett crossed the room to sit across from his father. Though the turmoil was building all too quickly inside, his face was calm. "I'm in love with her."

"Yes." Armand sat back. "I was afraid you were."

"I will not stand still and watch Deboque hurt someone else I love."

"Bennett, there are times, too many times, when our personal feelings can't influence our actions."

"For you." Bennett's voice was still calm, but slightly colder. "Perhaps for Alex as well, but not for me. I prefer to kill him myself."

Armand felt a ripple of fear, a tingle of pride and controlled both. "If you do anything to interfere with the operation at this point, you could be responsible for Hannah's death, not Deboque's."

Pushed to his limit, Bennett leaned forward. "Do you understand, I'm in love with her? If you were in my position, could you do nothing?"

Armand studied his son's face and remembered the only woman he'd ever loved. "I can only say that I would do whatever was necessary to keep her safe. Even if that meant doing nothing." He rose and went to his desk. "Read these." He lifted a small stack of files that carried the stamp of highest security. "These contain background information on Hannah, some of her own reports concerning certain assignments and most recently, her progress with

Deboque. I'll leave you so that you can read them here. They mustn't leave this room.''

Bennett rose to accept the files. "Where is she now?"

He had hoped the question wouldn't be asked. "She received a message early this morning. She's gone to Deboque.''

She had to play this one very carefully. Hannah sat with her hands folded on her lap in the elegant salon of Deboque's rented villa. Though the meeting was on land this time, she knew if her cover hadn't held up, she was just as much alone as she had been on the yacht.

If he had a hint of the part she'd played in the events of the evening before, her throat would be slit before she could voice a denial. A risk every agent takes, she reminded herself. To test herself, she lifted the small china pot on the table in front of her and poured coffee. Her hand was steady.

It was imperative that her mind stay sharp and focused on the assignment.

Every other thought in her mind was of Bennett.

"Lady Hannah." Deboque walked into the salon then shut the double doors at his back. "How delightful to see you again.''

She added a careful dollop of cream. "The message I received this morning left little option.''

"Ah, I was brusque." He crossed to her, taking her hand and brushing his lips over it. "My apologies. The events of last night caused me some distress.''

"And me." She drew her hand away. Instinct told her annoyance was the wisest course. "I find myself wondering if I've chosen wisely.''

Deboque chose the seat beside hers, then taking his time, chose a cigarette from a crystal holder. He wore emeralds today. "Meaning?"

"Only months ago, I found myself in the position of having to clean up for another of your employees." She sipped coffee. It was hot and Turkish. "Last night, another of them nearly ruined every carefully laid step I've taken toward the Bissets."

"May I remind you, *mademoiselle*, you were advised to stay out of the way?"

"I'll remind you, *monsieur*, that I haven't reached my current position by not looking toward my own interests. If I hadn't followed Bennett, you and I might even now be sitting in less agreeable quarters."

Deboque blew out smoke. "Explain."

"Bennett was a bit bored with the play and thought to wait in the American actress's dressing room until the curtain. Because I was aware that there were plans of some sort in the works, I decided it best to keep close. When the lights went out, I had to decide whether to go back or keep Bennett within reach. If I'd gone back, *monsieur*, the prince might indeed be dead."

"And for that you wish my gratitude?"

"He might be dead," Hannah repeated, "and a member of your organization would even now be in custody. Shall I pour you some coffee?"

"*Merci.*" He waited patiently while she filled a second cup. At his nod, she added cream.

Hannah sat back again and folded her ringless hands. "MacGee and the guards were already on their way. I spotted your man." She made a look of disgust. "He was bumbling his way around with a flashlight. I managed to distract Bennett by playing the hysterical female, but the idiot didn't take the opportunity to make good his escape. The lights came up again. Bennett saw him and his weapon. You should be flattered that since your release the prince has carried a small-caliber pistol with him. He used it, and for personal reasons, I'm grateful he used it well. Dead men can't name names.'' Playing up the role, she rose. "I ask you now, was the man under orders to kill one of the Bissets? Do you or do you not trust me to complete the contract?''

Say it! she ordered silently. Say it out loud, say it plainly so that this can be over.

Smoke curled up in a column toward the ceiling as he tapped the cigarette into an ashtray. "Please, my dear, be calm. The man you speak of may have been told to use initiative, but was never given a specific request. I have confidence in you, of course.''

"We agreed. I would dispose of the Bissets in return for five million dollars.''

He smiled, like a generous uncle. "We agreed that if such a thing were to happen, there would be some compensation.''

"I'm tired of playing games.'' As if to prove it, Hannah picked up her bag. "If you won't speak frankly, if you won't honor our arrangement, there's no reason to go on with this.''

"Sit.'' The order came sharp and clear as she walked to the door. Hannah stopped, turned, but didn't walk back. "You forget yourself. No one who works for me leaves until they are dismissed.''

She knew there would be men outside the door, to detain or dispose of her at Deboque's whim. She gambled that he would respect audacity. "Perhaps it's best if I find other employment then. I'm not accustomed to being dealt only half the cards.''

"Remember that I hold them. I ask you again, sit.''

This time she obeyed. She let the impatience shimmer, but only enough to let him see her control. "Very well.''

"Tell me how the Bissets cope this morning.''

"With dignity, of course.'' She pretended to be amused. "Bennett's pleased with himself. Armand is worried. Eve is confined to bed for the day. Gabriella stays with her. MacGee is closeted with Malori—you know the name?''

"Yes."

"I would guess that they are trying to see what purpose the disturbance last night had. Your man did an excellent job on the main power, though I think the explosive was a bit overstated.'' She shrugged as though it had been a hat with one too many feathers. "In any case, they ran on auxiliary for the rest of the evening and have a crew in the Center this morning for repairs. It's their belief that the power was blown so that the assassin could break his way into the Royal Box.''

"A natural assumption," Deboque said as he went back to his coffee. And exactly the one he'd hoped for. "Though such a move would have been messy and unstylish. And you, my dear? How do you cope after witnessing a killing?''

"I've chosen to be shocked and weakened by the events. But brave, naturally. We British are, you know.''

"I've always admired the quality.'' He smiled at her again. "I have to congratulate you on the depth of your skill. You look as though you didn't close your eyes all night.''

It was a mistake to remember, to think even for an instant, of Bennett. "I drank enough coffee to keep me awake until dawn," she said easily as her stomach tied itself in knots. "At the moment I'm supposedly out for a walk to clear my head.'' To take his attention from that, she added the last of what she and Reeve had discussed. "Are you aware that the entire Royal Family will gather at the palace for the Christmas Ball?''

"So is tradition.''

"With Eve being a bit delicate, the Princess Gabriella brings her family to stay for several days during the preparations. The MacGees share a wing with Alexander and Eve so that they can be close to the children.''

''Interesting.''

''And obliging. I'll require the makings for three plastic explosives.''

Deboque only nodded. ''The younger prince doesn't reside in the same wing.''

''The younger prince will be fatally injured while trying to save the rest of his family. Leave it to me. Just make sure the five million is waiting.'' She rose again, then inclined her head as if waiting for his permission to leave. Deboque stood as well, then surprised her by taking both of her hands.

''I had thought that some time after the holiday I would take a long vacation. I have an urge to sail, to be in the sun. Vacations can be very dull without companionship.''

Her stomach turned over. She prayed the revulsion wouldn't show, even for an instant. ''I've always been fond of the sun.'' She didn't object when he stepped closer, but smiled. ''You have a reputation for discarding women as easily as you collect them.''

''When they bore me.'' He cupped a hand around her neck. His fingers were light, smooth, and still made her think of spiders. ''I have a feeling you won't. I'm not attracted to looks, but brains and ambitions. Together, I believe we could be very comfortable.''

If his lips touched hers, she would retch. Knowing it, Hannah tilted her head back just an inch. ''Perhaps—after our business is completed.''

The fingers on her neck tightened, then released. The marks they had left wouldn't fade for several minutes. ''You're a cautious woman, Hannah.''

''Cautious enough to want the five million before I sleep with you. Now if you'll excuse me, I should get back before I cause any concern.''

''Of course.''

She walked to the door. "I'll need those supplies by the end of the week."

"Expect a Christmas present from your aunt in Brighton."

With a nod, she swung easily through the door.

Deboque took his chair again and decided he'd become quite fond of her. It was a shame she'd have to die.

Chapter Ten

It was midafternoon before Bennett went to find her. He'd read every word in the files Armand had given him. Though some had fascinated him, some had frightened him and some had angered him, he still wasn't sure he knew the woman.

Now he, too, was part of the deception, he thought as he made his way up to Eve's rooms. Nothing he'd read, nothing he'd been told could be confided to his brother. He couldn't comfort his sister or Eve with the fact that every move Deboque made was being monitored. He had, as he was coming to understand Hannah had, no choice but to play the game through. So he went to find her, knowing it was long past time they talked calmly.

He found Eve and Gabriella together at a table with piles of lists and a pot of tea.

"Bennett." Gabriella reached a hand out. "Just in time. We need a man's viewpoint on the Christmas Ball."

"Make sure there's plenty of wine." He bent to kiss both of her cheeks. Though she'd smiled at him, he'd recognized the signs of strain, just as he recognized them in Eve. "Hannah's not with you?"

"No." Eve set her pencil down as she lifted her face for Bennett's kiss. "I told her I wanted her to rest today. Last night..." She tightened her fingers on his. "Last night must have been dreadful for her. And you."

He shrugged, remembering too clearly the way he'd left her—curled into a silent ball on the bed. "It wasn't a dull evening in any case."

"Don't joke, Ben. You could have been killed. All I can think is that it's the second time in the theater. The second time one of my plays—"

Keeping Eve's hand in his, he crouched down. "I wasn't hurt, and I don't want you letting that fertile imagination go. I'd be very annoyed if my nephew were born with worry lines. Where's Marissa?"

"Napping."

He rubbed a thumb under her eyes. "You should do the same."

Annoyance replaced the strain, as he'd hoped. "Now you sound like Alex."

"God forbid. Where is he, anyway?"

"Meetings." She nervously traced her fingers over the papers. "Most of the day. Everything's been switched to his offices here because of—because security prefers it."

"Then you should relax." He covered her hand with his. "You should know by now the Bissets are indestructible. At the least you should be grateful he's tied up for a while, otherwise he'd be in here hovering over you."

She managed to smile. "You do have a point."

Rising, he grinned down at Gabriella. "I suppose we can trust you to keep her in line—though you're not looking your best, either."

"Chivalry is never dead with you around."

"What are brothers for?" He wanted to gather them both close and tell them that nothing and no one would ever hurt them again. Instead, he gave his sister's hair a tug. "Now I'll let you two get back to what I'm sure is fascinating work." He'd gotten no farther than the head of the stairs when Gabriella caught up with him. "Ben."

He turned, and though he was ready with a smile, her expression stopped it.

Gabriella looked back over her shoulder to be certain they were far enough away from Eve's office, then laid a hand over his on the banister. "Reeve tells me little about certain matters." A trace of temper came into her eyes, then was dismissed. "That's something I have to live with. But particularly since I once lost everything, I have very good instincts when it comes to my family."

"I know you're worried," he began. "All of us are."

"It's more than that, though everything comes back to Deboque and his obsession with destroying us. I still have dreams, even after all these years." She could remember a cabin, and the dark, and the fear.

"Brie." He laid a hand on her cheek. "Nothing like that is ever going to happen again."

She closed her fingers lightly over his wrist. "And I remember seeing you shot and bleeding on the terrace floor. I remember sitting in the hospital while Eve hung between life and death. Deboque." Her face was very pale, but there was strength in it and in the hand that lay on his. "It's all been Deboque. And he isn't finished."

"He will be." Something dangerous came into his voice, into his eyes. "That I promise you."

"I want you to be careful, Bennett."

He smiled, so that the look vanished. "How can I be otherwise with a dozen guards smothering me?"

"Very careful," she repeated. "I've never known you to carry a pistol to the theater."

She knew it was a lie. He didn't have to hear her say it, only to look in her eyes. She knew, but didn't understand. And because she was Gabriella, she wouldn't stop until she did.

"Leave it for now."

"So Reeve told me," she said with an impatient gesture. "It's my family. How can I?"

"I only know it's going to be over soon. In the meantime we have to stand together. Something's being done, Brie. Hold on to that."

"I have been." She knew it was unfair to push, so released him. "I want you to promise you won't do anything rash."

"What is this reputation I carry with me?"

"Ben, please."

"All right, you have it." He kissed her again. "I adore you, even if you did bring Dorian into the world to pester me." He gave her hand a final pat before he started down the stairs. *"A bientôt."*

She watched him go, but the worry stayed with her. *"A bientôt."*

Hannah wasn't in her rooms. Bennett found himself frustrated yet again when he entered and found them empty. Had she gone out again? he wondered. Was she even now putting herself in danger to protect his family?

He hated it. The thought of her risking her life, of blocking his body with her own as she had done last night was impossible to accept. Whether it was family, friend or country, he protected. How could he do less for the woman he loved?

Wandering in her rooms, he moved to her dresser. There was a small enameled box with a peacock on the lid. He ran a finger over it, wondering where she had come by it. A gift? From whom? A purchase in some little shop in London? He needed to know even those inconsequential details about her. Couldn't she understand that in order to resolve his feelings he had to know the woman he'd given them to?

He looked up, and reflected in the mirror was the bed where they'd fought, and loved, the night before. If he stood very still, he could almost feel the echoes of passion and discovery in the air. Would she hate him for that? Even though the loving had been as intense and as stunning for her as for him, would she forgive him for forcing her to set the barriers aside?

He'd been rough.... Bennett looked down at his own hands, turning them over, spreading his fingers. And he hadn't cared. All of his life he'd taken such pains never to hurt a woman. Now, when he'd found the only woman, he'd set out to do just so.

Walking to the window he stared out and tried to sort out his feelings. He still resented her. No matter what his brain told him, his heart was still bruised by the deception. More, he couldn't shake off the feeling that he'd fallen in love with two women and could trust neither.

Then he saw her in the gardens below.

She needed some time, Hannah told herself. Just an hour alone to clear her mind and calm her nerves. She knew she'd handled Deboque as smoothly as possible that morning. If nothing went wrong, they would close the trap on him in a week. Then she would have succeeded. In her file would go another favorable report. A two-year assignment successfully tied up could very well mean a promotion. She was, she knew, only inches away from a captaincy. Why didn't it excite her as it once had?

Time, Hannah told herself again. She just needed some time.

She would take a much needed and well earned vacation. Perhaps at last she would go to America—New York, San Francisco. Wouldn't it be possible to lose herself in such places for a while?

Or perhaps she would go back to England. She could spend time in Cornwall walking the moors or riding by the sea. In England she couldn't lose herself, but perhaps she could find herself again.

Wherever she went, she would be leaving Cordina. And Bennett.

Wisteria rose up in an arch, sheltering a bench and inviting long, lazy contemplations. She sat, and closing her eyes, tried to bring her troubled mind to rest.

Who was she? For the first time in years she was forced to ask herself and admit she didn't know the answer. A part of her was the quiet woman who enjoyed a long afternoon with a book, who liked to talk of literature and art. A part of her was the woman who kept a weapon within reach and listened to footsteps behind her.

The fact that she could be both had always been a benefit before, never, as it was now, a painful puzzle to solve. She wished she could talk with her father, even for an hour. He understood what it was to live two lives and find contentment and challenge in each.

But she couldn't risk even that. In this, as in the assignment that had brought her here, she was alone.

He detested her. It was Bennett who had caused the ache and the doubts. It was Bennett who had forced her to question what she'd always taken for granted. Last night he'd taken her mind and heart and body, only because he'd wanted to humiliate her. And he had. No one, no one had ever shown her how much there could be, how much she could give. No one had ever left her so empty and alone.

He wouldn't know how much he'd hurt her. He couldn't know, she thought as the tears she'd held off throughout the night began to fall. Because he would never know how strong her feelings were for him, and how hopeless.

She had chosen her path, Hannah reminded herself, and she would live with it. In a matter of days it would no longer cross his.

He would be safe. His family would be safe. And she would be gone.

He found her sitting on the bench, her hands folded neatly in her lap, her eyes closed and her face wet with tears. So many feelings tumbled into him that he couldn't separate them. Regret, confusion, love, guilt.

She'd want to be left alone. He thought he understood her that well. There was still enough bitterness in him to want to leave her alone. He could no more have left her there than he could have left a wounded dog on the side of the road.

As he went closer, Hannah sprang up from the bench. He saw the shock and humiliation run across her face. For a moment, he thought she would turn and run. But she held her ground.

"I thought I was alone." Her voice was cold as she fought anger and embarrassment.

He took out a handkerchief and offered it. At the moment it was the only comfort he could give, or she accept. "I'm sorry I disturbed you." His voice was as stiff as hers. "I think we need to talk."

"Haven't we?" She dried her face then crumpled the linen in her hands.

"Would you like to sit?"

"No, thank you."

He slipped his hands into his pockets. She hadn't slept, he thought as he saw the shadows under her eyes. Neither had he. So perhaps there they were even. "I spoke with my father this morning. You've met with Deboque already today."

She started to cut him off, but relented. The garden was as secure as the palace—for the moment. "I don't report to you on those matters, Your Highness."

Temper narrowed his eyes and balled his hands into fists, but he spoke evenly. "No, but I'm now fully aware of the situation. I read your files."

Her breath came out on a huff of air. Was nothing she was or had done hers alone any longer? "Very well then, your questions have been answered, your curiosity satisfied. You know everything there is to know about me—I hope you were entertained.''

"I didn't read it to be entertained," he tossed back. "Dammit, Hannah, I have a right to know."

"You have no rights where I'm concerned. I'm neither servant or subject."

"You're the woman I took to bed last night."

"That's best forgotten. Don't." Her body went rigid as he started forward. "Don't you ever touch me again."

"Very well." He stiffened even as she did. "But we both know certain things can't be forgotten."

"Mistakes can," she countered. "I'm here as an agent of the ISS to protect you and your family, to stop Deboque's plans to ruin Cordina and avoid the repercussions in Europe. Whatever has to be done to assure that, I'll do, but I will *not* let you humiliate me again." The tears started again, blinding her. "Oh, damn you, can't you leave me alone? Wasn't last night enough retribution for you?"

That snapped the very tenuous control he had on his own temper. He grabbed her arm, closing his fingers over the firm muscle. "Is that all it meant to you? Retribution? Can you stand here now and tell me you felt nothing, feel nothing? How accomplished a liar are you?"

"It doesn't matter what I felt. You wanted to punish me, and you did."

"I wanted to love you, and I did."

"Stop." That hurt, more than she was able to stand. She pushed him away only to be caught closer. The movement sent wisteria blossoms raining. "Do you think I couldn't see how much you hated me? You looked at me and made me feel vile. For ten years I've been proud of what I do, and you took even that away from me."

"And what of you?" He kept his voice low, but the anger was just as potent. "Can you tell me you didn't know I was in love with you?" She started to shake her head in denial, but he tightened his fingers. "You knew I was in love with a woman who didn't even exist. A quiet, shy and honest woman to whom I only wanted to show tenderness and patience. For the first time in my life there was a woman I could give my heart and my trust to, and she was nothing but a mirage."

"I don't believe you." But she wanted to and her heart began to race. "You were restless, even bored. I entertained you."

"I loved you." He lifted his hand and held her face very still, very close. She saw his eyes as she had the night before, tawny with passion. "You'll have to live with that."

"Bennett—"

"And when I came to your room last night, I found another woman, one who had lied and used me." He dragged the hand up, raking through her hair so that pins scattered. "One who looked like a witch," he murmured as her hair fell heavily over his hands. "And I wanted her just as badly, but without those tender, those sweet feelings. God help me, I still want her."

When his mouth came down on hers, she didn't protest. She'd also seen the truth in his eyes. He had loved her. Or he had loved the pretense of her. If desire was all he could give her now, she would take it. For duty she had sacrificed love, but even for duty, she wouldn't sacrifice the crumbs she had left.

She wrapped her arms around him. Perhaps if she could give him the passion, some day he would forgive her the rest.

How easily he could lose himself in her. The passion was edgy and achy but it didn't seem to matter. Her mouth was warm, her body slender and straining. If it wasn't love she felt for him, at least there was need. He'd settled for no more than that before.

"Tell me you want me," he demanded as he moved his mouth desperately over her face.

"Yes, I want you." She hadn't known it possible to feel triumph and defeat at the same time.

"Come with me now."

"Bennett, I have no right to this." She turned her face into his throat, wanting to draw just a little more of him into her. "I'm here only because—"

With his hands on her shoulders he drew her away before she could finish the denial. "For today, for one day, we'll put your duty and mine aside."

"And tomorrow?"

"Tomorrow comes whether we want it to or not. Give me a few hours, Hannah."

She would have given him her life, and somehow knew that would be easier than what he was asking now. Still, she put her hand in his.

They went on horseback. As Hannah cantered beside him, she could see that Bennett knew the route to their destination well. They turned into the woods where they'd raced once before, and he took the lead. Each time doubts rose up to plague her, she beat them back. She would take the few hours she was being offered.

She heard the stream before she saw it. It was a simple, musical sound that suited the leafy shade and towering trees. When Bennett came to it, he turned his horse south. For a quarter of a mile they rode along the bank in silence.

The stream curved and twisted, then widened at a point where a trio of willows draped over it. Bennett stopped there and swung from the saddle.

"What a lovely spot." Hannah reined in, but found herself not quite courageous enough to dismount. "Every time I think I've seen the most beautiful place in Cordina, I find another. Do you often come here?"

"Not often enough." He'd secured his horse and now walked to her. Saying nothing, he held up a hand.

Here was the choice he'd refused to give her the night before. Perhaps he gave it to her now because he knew the decision had already been made. Hannah curled her fingers into his, held a moment, then dismounted. The silence continued while she tethered her horse beside his.

"I came here when my mother died." He didn't know why it seemed important that he tell her. "Not to grieve really, but because she always loved places like this. See the little white flowers along the bank?" His hand was on hers again as they moved closer to the stream. "She called them angel wings. They're sure to have a complicated Latin name, but angel wings seemed right."

Bending, he plucked one. It was no bigger than his thumb with thin petals cupped around a tiny blue center. "Every summer, before I'd have to go back to Oxford, I'd come here. For some reason it made leaving easier." He tucked the flower into her hair. "When I was a child, I thought the fairies lived here. I used to look for them in the clover and under toadstools."

She smiled and touched a hand to his cheek. "Did you ever find one?"

"No." With his hand on her wrist, he turned his head to press his lips to her palm. "But I think they're still here. That's why this place is magic. That's why I want to make love with you here."

Their lips were still an inch apart as they lowered to the grass. They remained a breath apart as they began to undress each other. Kneeling, gazes locked, they unfastened buttons. Sunlight dappled over skin as material was pushed aside. Their lips brushed, then clung.

He couldn't stop the rush of power, the flood of need. In seconds they were rolling over the grass. He caressed her everywhere, seeking, finding, exploiting until her moans shuddered into his mouth. The need to take her quickly, fiercely, couldn't be fought down, especially when her fingers were already tugging at the clasp of his jeans.

They waited only until all barriers were removed, then joined in a rocketing, furious journey that left them both sated.

Naked, with the grass tickling her back, Hannah looked up at the sunlight filtering through the leaves overhead. It had been moonlight before and she'd experienced a range of feelings from anger, shame, ecstasy and back to shame again. Today, in the sunlight, she no longer felt the shame.

What was between them could be, for this short time, between the man and the woman. Tomorrow they would be prince and agent again.

"What are you thinking?"

She was able to smile and turn her head toward him. "That this is a beautiful spot."

He'd wanted to bring her there before. He'd imagined it. How he would slowly, patiently, show her the pleasures of loving. Shaking off the mood, he drew her closer. This was a different day, and a different woman. "Are you warm enough?"

"Hmmm. But I..." she trailed off, knowing she'd sound foolish.

"But?"

"Well, I've never—" How to phrase it? "I've never lain naked in the grass under the sun before."

He laughed, not even realizing that the tone and the feeling behind it had come from the woman he'd first known. "Life should always include new experiences."

"I'm sure you've found yourself naked in all manner of unusual places."

The dry voice delighted him. Rolling over, he pressed a kiss to her mouth then drew back just to look at her. Her hair was fanned out over the dark grass. The tiny white flower was tangled in it as though it had grown there. Bruising shadows under her eyes made her look both wanton and delicate, as though she were a virgin who'd just spent a night being initiated into womanhood.

This was how he had once imagined her, how he had once wanted, how he had once loved.

"You're so beautiful."

She smiled, relaxed enough to be amused. "Now *that* I've never been."

He traced a fingertip along her cheekbone. "How unobservant of you, Hannah. Or how foolish. Making yourself look less attractive doesn't change the truth. Flawless skin." He traced his lips over it as if to taste. "These elegant bones that make a man wonder if you're made of flesh and bone or glass. Those calm, intelligent eyes that drove me mad wondering how they might darken and cloud if I could find the right way to touch you. And this." He rubbed a finger over her lips. "So soft, so generous." He lowered his head but only traced the shape with his tongue. "Do you remember the first time I kissed you?"

Her breath was already shaking, her eyes already closing. "Yes. I remember."

"I wondered how it was that such a quiet woman could make my knees weak with just a taste."

"Kiss me now," she demanded and drew him down to her.

It wasn't what she expected. There was tenderness instead of passion, patience rather than urgency. She murmured against his mouth in confusion. Bennett only stroked his fingers over her face and waited for her to relax. More, he waited for her to accept. Even when he deepened the kiss it remained gentle. The fire was there but smoldering rather than blazing.

He was making love to the Hannah he'd understood, she realized and wanted to weep. There was lust for one, affection for the other. How could she fight another woman when the woman was herself?

On a trembling sigh, she let her mind empty. She would give him whatever it was he needed today.

He felt the change—the slow, almost fluid surrender. With a murmured approval, he pressed his lips to her throat. He wanted to show her there could be more than flash and speed. If they only had a few hours, then he would use them to give her whatever sweetness she would accept from him.

Lightly he stroked the smoothness of her body. What he'd demanded from her the night before, he now requested, coaxed, offered. He took the time to watch her arousal grow as the sun filtered down on her face and the stream rushed by beside them. He murmured to her as he kissed her throat. There were promises, endearments, reassurances. She answered him in words so fragile they almost dissolved in the air.

She'd never been loved like this before—as though she was precious, as though she was special. Even with her mind fogging over she could hear the gentle hiss of water running over rock. She could smell the grass and the wild sweet flowers scattered through it. With her eyes half-opened, the sunlight seemed gold and bountiful over her lover's skin. She ran her hand over it, finding it smooth and taut and warm.

Her lover. Hannah brought his mouth back to hers and gave him everything that was in her heart. If the place was magic, then so was the moment. Dreams hadn't been a part of her life for too long to remember, but she opened herself to them now.

She was so giving, so pliant. He'd wanted too badly to feel this kind of emotion from her. It went far beyond heat, far above desire. She touched him as though she'd been waiting for him all of her life. She kissed him as though he were her first and only lover. The more she gave, the more he found in himself to give back. The shadows shifted and lengthened over them as they stroked and offered and discovered.

Even when he slipped into her, it was slow and easy. The passion that had built was still harnessed by stronger emotions. They moved together in a harmony that seemed almost painful in its perfection while she framed his face with her hands and his lips met hers.

They glided over the top and settled softly.

"You wanted to see me, Monsieur Deboque?"

"Yes, Ricardo." Deboque lifted his teapot and poured. He admired the British habit of tea in the late afternoon. It was so civilized. "I have a little shopping list for you." With one hand he gestured toward the desk by the window. "I'd like you to supervise it personally."

"Of course." Always pleased to be given trust, Ricardo picked up the list written on heavy cream-colored paper. His brow lifted only a fraction. "Shall I requisition this from within the company?"

"Please." Deboque added cream to his tea. "I prefer to keep this at home, so to speak. The delivery should be set up with Lady Hannah on...Thursday, I'd say. It's no use passing the merchandise along to her too soon."

"She risks much, smuggling such a—volatile package into the palace."

"I have implicit trust in our British friend, Ricardo." He remembered the way she'd sat across from him that morning. Trim, tidy and cultured. It gave his plans such a pleasant touch when they were carried out by delicate hands. "She has a certain style, wouldn't you say?"

"Class, even when so quietly cloaked, is still class, *monsieur*."

"Precisely." Deboque smiled and sipped at his tea. "I have no doubt she will carry out her objective with class."

He sipped his tea again and sighed. "I do admire the British, Ricardo. So traditional, so resilient. Not as passionate as the French, but so wonderfully pragmatic. In any case, see that the merchandise is shipped from the address on that list. I don't wish it to come through my hands."

"Of course."

"I'm preparing an itinerary, Ricardo. We'll be sailing the end of next week. I'll see Lady Hannah once more. You'll see to the details?"

"As you wish."

"Thank you, Ricardo. Oh, by the way, did you see that a wreath was sent to Bouffe's funeral?"

"Roses as you requested, *monsieur.*"

"Excellent." Deboque chose one of the little sugared biscuits from the Wedgwood plate. "You're very dependable."

"I try, *monsieur.*"

"Have a pleasant evening then, Ricardo. Do let me know if we get any further word on the accident at the theater. I'm very uncomfortable with the current report."

"I will. Good evening, *monsieur.*"

Deboque sat back, nibbling on the cookie. Ricardo continued to please him a great deal. An intelligent man with sociopathic tendencies was an excellent addition to his staff. Deboque was certain Ricardo would be very grateful to have the assignment of dealing with Hannah when her job was completed. It was tempting, but Deboque discarded it.

He would deal with Hannah himself. After all, the least he could do after she'd given him his fondest wish was to see she died as painlessly as possible.

Chapter Eleven

Hannah appeared very calm as she sipped tea in the library. She listened to Reeve give an updated report to Malori, filling in occasionally when requested to, then lapsing back into silence.

Bennett had started to show her the library once. Then they'd detoured into the music room. And he'd kissed her. Was that when her life had really begun to change? she wondered. Had it been then, or the day on the beach when he'd given her a shell? Perhaps it had been that first night in the gardens.

"Do you agree, Hannah?"

She snapped back, cursing herself for letting her mind wander at such a crucial time. They had only thirty minutes for the briefing, half of which was already gone. Even within the walls of the palace it was dangerous for them to meet.

"I'm sorry. Could you repeat that?"

Armand had been watching her, wondering if her shoulders were strong enough to hold the fate of so much. "The last few days have been a strain." There wasn't criticism in his voice but concern. Hannah would have preferred the first.

"The last two years have been a strain, Your Highness." Then she lifted her shoulders in a gesture that was more acceptance than dismissal.

"If you're beginning to wear under it," Malori said in his clipped, no-nonsense voice, "it's best we know now."

"I don't wear." Her eyes met his without wavering. "I believe my record shows that."

Before Malori could speak again, Reeve cut in. She was wearing, he knew, but he had to gamble she'd hold out for a few more days. "If we could backtrack? We can assume that Deboque has already ordered the supplies you requested. An educated guess on where he'd procure them?"

"Athens," she said immediately. "I feel strongly that he'd draw from within his own organization. He feels totally secure, invulnerable if it comes to that. He wouldn't want to risk ordering from outside sources. From my other reports, we know that he keeps a warehouse in Athens. He has others, of course, but I think he'd go there because of its proximity to Cordina."

"We'll check our contact there and see if there's news of any explosives being moved." Malori noted it down. "With luck we'll close down his Athens branch once we have him here."

"The ISS won't move on Athens, Paris, London or Bonn until we have an airtight case on Deboque here." Hannah set down her tea. "That's a button I push, *monsieur*."

"*Bien.*" Malori obviously didn't like it, but nodded.

"Will the case be strong enough when Hannah receives the explosives?" Armand glanced at Hannah, then at Reeve. "Hannah has taken the contract, requested the supplies. Once they are delivered, can that be the end of it?"

Hannah started to speak, then subsided. She would let Reeve explain. He was family. "We would have enough for an arrest, possibly for an arraignment. Even with the supplies being traced back to Athens or another of Deboque's companies, it wouldn't be enough for a conspiracy conviction. He's careful enough to divorce himself from business dealings of this kind."

Business dealings, Armand thought as he drummed his fingers on the arm of the chair. "And his request that Hannah assassinate my family?"

"His hypothetical theory of what might happen if such a thing occurred," Reeve corrected. "Your Highness, I'm aware, very aware, of the frustration of not being able to close in on the evidence we have now. We had him once for over a decade, and it didn't stop him. If we want to crush Deboque once and for all, sever all these strings and hack away his control in Europe, we have to have solid and indisputable evidence of murder and conspiracy. Hannah will give us that in a matter of days."

Armand drew out a cigarette and shifted his gaze to Hannah. "How?"

"The payoff." She felt herself on solid ground again. It helped to have Malori there, sharp-eyed and just a bit disapproving. "When Deboque is convinced I've completed the job, he'll pay me off. As soon as money changes hands, we've got him."

"He's not a fool. You agree?"

"No, Your Highness, he's not a fool."

"But you will convince him you have murdered my family."

"Yes. If you would look at this diagram, sir?" She rose and waited for him to accompany her to a table. With Reeve's help, she stretched out a long roll of paper. "The blueprints I smuggled to Deboque show this wing as occupied by Prince Alexander and his family. I gave Deboque the information that Princess Gabriella and her family would also be staying here during the days before the Christmas Ball."

"I see. In truth, my son's family's wing is here." He skimmed his finger to the opposite side of the drawing.

"The night before the ball, I'll set some charges here, and here." She laid a fingertip on the areas. "They'll be much

smaller than what Deboque assumes, but with Reeve's special effects added, it should be quite a show. There will be
some damage, sir, but it will appear much worse, particu-
arly from the outside, than it really is. You'll need to do
some replastering and painting.''

He lifted a brow, but she couldn't tell if he was amused.
'There are areas of the palace that could do with some re-
decorating.''

"It will be imperative, of course, to clear this wing. Discreetly.''

"Of course.''

"Ten minutes before the explosion, I will leave to meet
with Deboque or his agent. The payment will be made after
he considers the job done.''

"Have you considered that he would want to have the
deaths verified before he pays you?''

"Yes.'' Hannah straightened away from the diagram.
"To some extent we'll use the press. In addition, I'm making it clear that payment must be made that night, as well as
arrangements for my passage out of the country. Deboque
has invited me to sail with him. I shall accept.'' She pressed
her lips together as Malori grumbled. "The money will
change hands because he'll believe I'll be easily accessible if
anything has gone wrong.''

"And will you be?''

"I'll be with him.''

"The ISS will be covering both Deboque's villa and his
yacht,'' Reeve cut in. "The moment we have Hannah's signal, we move.''

"There is no other way?''

Again there was concern. This time Hannah found herself laying a hand on the prince's arm. On the arm of Bennett's father. "We could perhaps tie him to other crimes.
With the information I've been able to dig up in the last two
years, we would have something, but it would take months,

even years and we would have no guarantee. This is the only way, Your Highness, to stop him once and for all."

With a nod, the prince looked over at Reeve. "You agree?"

"Yes."

"Malori?"

"It is more dramatic, and certainly more risky than one would like, but yes, Your Highness."

"Then I will presume that you two will see to whatever details have yet to be seen to. I will expect reports every four hours."

Recognizing dismissal Malori bowed. Even as Reeve rolled up the diagram again, Hannah was preparing to curtsy.

"Hannah, I'd like another moment, please."

"Yes, Your Highness." She stood by the table, stiff and tense as the two other men left them alone. He would know of her feelings for Bennett, Hannah thought. Even in the brief time she'd been in Cordina, she'd learned that Armand was both astute and observant. He didn't merely rule from a throne, but behind a desk and in boardrooms. If his country was at peace and prosperous, it was largely because he knew how to govern, how to make choices and how to remain objective.

Yes, he would know, she thought again. And he would not approve. She was European. She was an aristocrat. But she was by choice and by profession a spy.

"You're uncomfortable," Armand began. "Sit, please."

In silence she took a seat and waited.

She looked like a dove, he thought. A small gray dove who expected and accepted the fact that she was about to be mauled by a fox. Studying her, he had difficulty believing she would be the one to end the turmoil that had haunted his family for more than a decade.

"Reeve has confidence in you."

"I can promise it's not misplaced, Your Highness." She nearly relaxed. It wasn't about Bennett, but Deboque.

"Why did you agree to take this assignment?"

Her brow lifted because it seemed such a simple question with such a simple answer. "I was asked."

"And had the right to refuse?"

"Yes, sir. In such matters an agent always has a choice."

A prince didn't. He understood the difference, yet still didn't envy her. "You took the assignment because your superiors requested it."

"Yes, and because what Deboque does here has affected and could continue to affect my country and the rest of Europe. A terrorist, in whatever garb he chooses, remains a terrorist. England wants Deboque's hands tied, tightly."

"Your first consideration is country."

"It always has been."

He nodded again, knowing this could bring both joy and misery. "Did you choose your profession because you looked for adventure?"

Now she relaxed completely and laughed. The moment she did, Armand saw what had captivated his son. "Pardon, sir, I realize that the word 'spy' conjures up all sorts of glamorous images: foggy docks, Parisian alleyways, nickel-plated revolvers and fast cars. In truth, it's often tedious. In the past two years, I've done more work on telephones and computers than the average secretary."

"You wouldn't deny the danger involved."

"No." She sighed a little. "No. But for every hour of danger, there's a year of legwork and preparation. As for Deboque—Reeve, Malori, the ISS, have taken this plan step-by-step."

"Still, in the end, you'll be alone."

"That's my job. I'm good at it."

"Of that I have no doubt. Under normal circumstances, I would worry less."

"Your Highness, I assure you everything that can be done is being done."

He was aware of the truth of it and that, for the moment, his hands were tied. "And if a mistake is made, how will I comfort my son?"

She locked her fingers together. "I know, I promise you whatever happens, Deboque will be punished. "If you—"

"I'm not speaking of Deboque now, but of you, and of Bennett." He held up a hand before she could speak again. "It is a rare thing for me to be able to speak as only a father. I ask you to allow me that luxury now, here in this room."

She drew in a breath and tried to be clear. "I realize Bennett is angry and upset because he wasn't told the reasons for my being here. I believe he feels a certain responsibility toward me because I'm here to protect his family."

"He's in love with you."

"No." The panic set in again, along with the shame and the desperate desire for it to be true. "That is, he thought before when he believed me to be... At one time he began to feel a certain affection, but when he learned who—what I was, that changed."

Armand settled his hands on the arms of his chair. The ring of his office glinted in the lamplight. "My dear, are you any more clear on your feelings for him?"

She looked up. The dark eyes that watched her were kinder than they had been. Hard yes, he could be hard. But she could see now why his family and his country loved and trusted him. "Your confidence, sir?"

"You have it, of course."

"I love him more than I've ever loved anything or anyone. If I could change things, if I could go back and be what he thought I was, and only that, I swear to you I would." There were no tears. She had shed them once and had sworn not to do so again. Instead she looked down at her hands. "Of course, I can't."

"No, we can't change what we are. When we love, and love deeply, we can accept a great deal. Bennett's heart is very generous."

"I know. I promise you, I won't hurt him again."

His lips curved. She was so young, so valiant. "I have no fear of that. When this is done, I ask that you remain in Cordina for a few more days."

"Your Highness, I think it would be best if I returned to England immediately."

"We wish you to remain," he said again, and he no longer spoke as a father. He rose then, extending a hand. "You may want to rest before dinner."

Left without a choice, Hannah stood and curtsied. "Thank you, Your Highness."

Dinner was long and formal. Hannah was introduced to the Minister of State and his wife, as well as a German businessman who had interests in shipping and an ancient Frenchwoman who was some vague connection of the Bissets' and was visiting Cordina for the holidays. The Frenchwoman spoke in a husky grumble that kept Hannah straining to hear enough to make polite answers. The German spoke in short, loud blasts and was obviously delighted to have an invitation to the Royal Palace. Hannah was grateful that he was across the table so that she could avoid direct conversation with him.

Bennett wasn't there at all. A late board meeting at the museum had edged into a dinner for the Equestrian Society. Hannah tried to remember that Claude had been joined by two more guards who would keep Bennett annoyed and protected throughout the evening.

As the Frenchwoman hissed in her ear again, Hannah could only think Bennett the fortunate one.

Across the table, Eve sipped sparkling water and listened with apparent fascination as the German regaled her with stories of his business. Only when she turned to pick up her dessert spoon did her eyes meet Hannah's long enough for the humor to come through. Answering a question in low, polite tones, she rolled her eyes once, quickly, in a gesture that said everything. Then she was smiling at the German again and making him feel fascinating.

Hannah had to lift her glass to hide the grin. The royal were human after all. Not the same, not ordinary, but human. The child Eve carried might one day rule, but he would also laugh and cry and feel and dream.

She herself had loved a prince. Hannah picked up her spoon and began to toy with the elegant chocolate and cream concoction in front of her. She'd given her heart to a man who was second in line to one of the few remaining thrones in Europe. In a few days, she could very likely give her life for him.

For that was the truth of the matter, she thought as the woman beside her droned on. It might have started as duty, to her country and to the organization she had chosen, but when it ended, what she did would be for Bennett.

It would never be possible to tell him, just as it hadn't been possible to say as much to his father earlier that evening. If she admitted what she felt to a superior, even with all the planning, all the time lost, she could very well be pulled out.

So she would say nothing, but she would feel. And feeling as she did, she would see Deboque finished, if she lived.... And then, Hannah admitted, it would be a choice between her captaincy and retirement. Fieldwork would be all but out of the question now. She didn't believe that she could ever maintain the pose of quiet, unassuming Lady Hannah again. Not now that she had loved and been loved by a prince.

* * *

It was nearly midnight before escape could be politely made. Hannah deliberated over a hot bath or quick oblivion in bed as she stepped into her room. Eve was insistent about returning to the Center the next day, so she would have no choice but to go along. Would the message come the next day, or would Deboque take her right down to the wire?

She'd walked into the center of the bedroom when the warning signals began to throb at the base of her neck. There was no one in the room. A quick glance showed her nothing had been disturbed. But...

Hannah took a cautious step back and opened the drawer of the bedside table. She took out her weapon. The light was low and at her back as she began to move toward the adjoining room. The door was slightly ajar, but that could have been done by one of the maids. Her feet were silent on the carpet as she crossed to it. With one hand she pressed on the panel so that it opened slowly and without sound.

There was nothing in the room beyond—nothing except the neat sitting room that smelled of the gardenias that lay moist and lovely in a bowl.

So it had been a maid, she thought, relaxing gradually. One of them had set fresh flowers in the sitting room, and—

It was then she heard a sound, material against material, and tensed again. Keeping the gun secure in her hand, she slid against the wall and into the room.

The little settee faced away from the door so she didn't see him until she was fully inside. Bennett lay sprawled on it, his tie unknotted and hanging, his shoes off and his face buried in a blue velvet pillow.

Hannah swore, but softly, as she lowered the pistol. He looked exhausted, and very much at home, she thought as she lifted a brow. Her first instinct was to tuck a cover around him, but there was still enough of the proper Lady Hannah in her to know that it would never do for Bennett of Cordina to be found snoozing in her sitting room. She started to bend down to him, then remembered the gun in her hand.

Almost curiously, she turned it over in her hand. It looked like a toy, but had already proven itself lethal. A part of her job, she thought. A part of her life. Yet she knew it was a part Bennett would find unpalatable. Moving back into her bedroom she secured it. She had to wake him and send him on his way, but she didn't have to keep a physical reminder of their differences close at hand.

She went back to him, and kneeling by the settee put a hand to his shoulder. "Bennett." She shook gently and received a mumbled response. Her lips curved. She had to resist the urge to brush at the hair tumbling over his forehead. In sleep, the energy, the amusement and the temper were put to rest. He looked as though he would be perfectly content to cuddle there, half on, half off the little sofa for days. Hannah bent closer and raising her voice gave him a quick, brisk shove. "Bennett, wake up."

He half opened his eyes, but Hannah noted that they focused quickly. Reaching up, he grabbed her earlobe. "Haven't you any respect for a dead man?"

"Ow!" She grabbed his wrist in defense, but she was already several inches closer. "If it's respect you want, I'll call a couple of the servants and have them carry you out, in state. Meanwhile, let go or I'll have to show you how easy it is to cause unconsciousness by applying pressure to certain nerves."

"Hannah, you've got to learn not to be so flighty and romantic."

"It's in the blood." She sat back on her heels to massage her ear. "Bennett, why are you sleeping on my settee instead of in your own bed?"

"I don't know who designed this thing. Another foot longer and a man could be comfortable." He dragged himself up a bit so that his feet dangled over the arm. "I wanted to talk to you." He rubbed both hands over his face. "When I got in, I saw that we still had guests. I took the coward's way and used the back stairs."

"I see. And Madame Beaulieu spoke so highly of you."

"Madame Beaulieu doesn't speak, she hisses."

"I know. I sat next to her at dinner."

"Better you than me."

"How gallant."

"You want gallant?" With one swing, he had her off the floor and stretched on top of him. He cupped the back of her neck with his hand, pressing as his mouth took hers quickly, completely.

"What does that have to do with gallantry?" she managed after a moment.

He smiled and ran a finger down her nose. "All the other women I've known have been impressed by it."

Hannah drew back another inch. Smiling, she ran a finger down his throat, then up again. "About those nerves I mentioned."

He caught one wrist, then the other. "All right then, tomorrow I'll look for a puddle to toss a cape over."

"A safe enough promise since it hasn't rained in days." She started to shift, but he brought her close again.

"Stay. I haven't seen you at all today." His lips were warm and coaxing against her cheek. "Do you know, Hannah, a man has to have you in his arms, has to have his lips against your skin before he catches your scent. Do you do that on purpose?"

She wore no perfume. It had to do with leaving no traces behind. "You said you..." He moved his lips to her ear. "You wanted to talk to me."

"I lied." His teeth closed gently over her earlobe. "I wanted to make love with you. In fact, I had a devil of a time keeping my mind off that thought throughout a long and frustrating board meeting and a noisy dinner." He drew down the zipper at the back of her dress. "I had to give a speech." He found silk, thin, fragile silk, beneath the linen. "It was difficult not to babble when I kept imagining myself here, with you."

"I don't want to interfere with your official duties." With her eyes closed, she pressed her lips to his neck and let herself enjoy the gentle stroking of his hands.

"But you do, *ma mie*. I sat listening to the huffing and puffing of ten stuffy men who are more interested in paintings than people, and I imagined you sitting there with your hands neatly folded and your eyes solemn. And you were wearing nothing but your hair."

She'd slipped off his tie, but paused now on the third button of his shirt. "In the boardroom?"

"In the boardroom." Would he ever stop being fascinated by that dry, serious tone and those dark eyes? "You can see why I had such a problem concentrating." He didn't tell her he'd also dealt with unexpected tingles of fear as he'd pictured her with Deboque, at his mercy, helpless, alone. It was an image he hadn't been able to drown out in innumerable cups of coffee or glasses of wine. "So I came in here to wait for you."

"And fell asleep."

"I'd hoped you'd see the irony and reverse the fairy tale. Wake the sleeping prince with a kiss. Instead I got a shove."

With her hands framing his face, she drew his head up. "Let me make up for it now then."

She touched her lips to his, brushed, retreated, teased then touched again. She felt him tense his fingers at her back as she toyed with his mouth. Her tongue traced, her teeth nipped as heat built to a flash point. She didn't object when he pressed her head closer, when his mouth closed hungrily over hers. If he had longed for her through the day, his need had been no sharper than her own. They would take the night hours together.

She had his shirt unbuttoned and open. Her dress had slipped down, revealing the shimmer of honey-colored lace beneath. Bennett let his fingertips play over it while he absorbed the contrasts and delights that were his Hannah. He drew the pins out of her hair so that it flowed over her shoulders and his. The scent of it was as light and elusive as the scent of her skin. What witchery she had was an innate part of her rather than something that came from bottles and pots.

Fresh, real, his. Delirious from her, he tugged the dress down her body and let it fall to the rug.

And his fingers slid over the stiletto strapped to her thigh.

She stiffened, remembering the weapon the instant he discovered it. Passion cooled so swiftly, she shivered. When she drew away he didn't stop her.

"Bennett, I'm sorry." She'd forgotten there could be no apologies, no regret. His eyes were on hers, blank and flat, as he sat up. Because there was nothing for her to say, no way for her to remove the barrier, she lapsed into silence.

Her hair was a riot of honey-toned waves that fell over her shoulders and the silk that echoed the color. Her eyes, darkly, richly green, were solemn now as she waited for him to speak. Or to leave.

Fighting the first stirrings of anger, he let his gaze pass over her, the milk-pale skin, the slender curves, the delicate silk. She was what she'd convinced herself she was not— beautiful, stunning, desirable. On one long slim thigh strapped by thin strong leather, was a knife associated with dark alleys and smoky bars. Saying nothing, Bennett reached for it. She automatically caught his wrist.

"Bennett—"

"Be quiet." His voice was as flat and cool as his eyes. Hannah let her fingers fall away. Slowly, he drew the weapon from its sheath. It was warmed from her skin, small enough to fit into the palm of his hand. Until he pushed the button and the thin blade slid silently, lethally out. It caught the lamplight and glistened silver.

She wore it intimately, he thought. He wanted to ask her if she'd used it, but a part of him knew it was best to keep the question to himself for now. It weighed nothing, but sat heavy as lead in his hand.

"Why do you need this in the palace?"

She pushed a strap back onto her shoulder, then rubbed the skin there that was growing colder and colder. "I'm expecting word from Deboque. I can't be sure when or where it will come from. Because I may have to respond to it immediately, it's best to be prepared."

"What kind of word?"

"I think you should ask—"

"I'm asking you." His voice carried a lash he used rarely, but effectively. "What kind of word, Hannah?"

Hannah drew her knees up to her chest, wrapped her arms around them and told him everything. There could be no objection now, she reminded herself. He already knew too much.

"So we sacrifice a part of the east wing. Camouflage." He twisted the blade under the light. He knew, without doubt, he could have plunged it into Deboque's heart.

"The more genuine things seem, the more easily Deboque will be convinced. He won't part with five million dollars until he's sure Cordina is left without an heir."

"He would kill the children," Bennett murmured. "Even Alexander's unborn child. All for what? Revenge, power, money?"

"For all three. He would have his revenge on your father, his own power would grow from the chaos, and money would follow. It's his greed that will topple him this time, Bennett. I promise you."

It was the passion in her voice that had him looking at her again. Her eyes were wide and dry, but the emotion almost leapt from them. To protect his family, he thought as he tightened his hand on the handle of the stiletto. To protect herself. As suddenly as he'd fallen in love, he realized the full truth. Whatever she did, whatever she used didn't matter, as long as she kept herself safe.

He pressed the release and sent the blade back home. And he would see to that himself. After setting the knife aside, he reached over to unsnap the strap from her thigh. Her skin had gone cold, he discovered, though the room was warm. It stirred something in him that he recognized again as a need to protect. She didn't move, didn't speak and flinched only slightly when he rose. She was waiting for him to reject her, to dismiss her, to leave her.

He felt both her surprise and her doubt as he gathered her up into his arms. "You should trust me more, Hannah," he said quietly.

When she relaxed against him, when she let her head rest on his shoulder, he carried her to bed.

Chapter Twelve

The package was delivered in the most pedestrian of ways. It was carried by Dartmouth Shippers, one of Deboque's less profitable but most useful tentacles. It was marked with the return address of Hannah's aunt in England and stamped FRAGILE.

The only difficulty came from the fact that Eve was present when it was delivered.

"Oh, what fun!" Eve hovered around the package. "It's a Christmas present, isn't it? Why don't you open it?"

"It isn't Christmas," Hannah said mildly, and set the package on the shelf in her closet. She would turn it over to Reeve at the first opportunity.

"Hannah, how can you be so casual about it?" With nerves just below the surface, Eve poked around the room. "Didn't you ever search under beds and in closets for packages at this time of year?"

"No." Hannah smiled and went back to arranging the flowers Eve had brought her. "I never wanted to spoil Christmas morning."

"It doesn't spoil it, it only adds to the excitement." Eve glanced back at the closet. "Couldn't we just peek?"

"Absolutely not, though I can tell you the package probably contains five dozen homemade cookies—as hard as bricks. Aunt Honoria is nothing if not predictable."

"It doesn't feel like Christmas." Moody, Eve wandered to the window. She laid one hand protectively over the swell of her belly and fidgeted nervously at the curtain with the other. "The ballroom's being scrubbed and polished for the holiday, the tree's already trimmed. If I walk by the kitchens there are the most glorious scents, but it just doesn't feel like Christmas."

"Are you homesick, Eve?"

"Homesick?" Puzzled for a moment, she turned around, then smiled. "Oh, no. Alex and Marissa are here. I do hope my sister manages to get away from her art gallery for a week or two, but I don't miss the States really. It's just that everyone tries to pamper me, protect me by hiding things." Sighing, she moved to Hannah's dresser to toy with the little enameled box Bennett had admired. "I know how tense and worried Alex is, no matter how hard he tries to pretend everything's fine. Even when I talk to Bennett, his mind only seems to be half with me. It has to stop, Hannah. I can't bear to see the people I love torn apart this way."

She too would pamper, and protect by hiding things, but it was the only comfort Hannah could allow herself to give. "It's this Deboque, isn't it?"

Eve set the box down again. "How can one man bear so much hate? How can one man cause so much pain? I know, though after years I still can't really understand, I know that he won't be satisfied until he's destroyed us."

"It isn't possible for most of us to understand real evil," Hannah began, though she could and did understand it. "But I think we only add to it when we let our lives be affected so strongly."

"You're right, of course." Eve held out both hands. "Do you know how grateful I am that you're here? Without you I'm afraid I'd be moody and brooding all of the time. Brie's coming later today with all the children. We still have florists and musicians to deal with." She squeezed Hannah's hands as she drew a deep breath. "I hate being helpless. What I'd like to do is to go up and spit in Deboque's eye, but if all I can do is make things easier here, then I'll have to be content with that.''

Hannah vowed, at the first opportunity, to spit in De-boque's eye for her. ''Why don't you take me up to the ballroom and show me what's been done? I'd like to help.'' She wanted to help—and she wanted Eve away from the package that sat on the shelf in the closet.

''All right, but I want you to come to my room first. I have a present for you.''

''Presents are for Christmas,'' Hannah reminded her as they walked to the door.

''This one can't wait.'' She had to get her mind off the undercurrents that were pressing in on them all. Dr. Franco had already warned her that her tension could affect the child. ''Pregnant princesses must be indulged.''

''How clever of you to use that to your advantage when it suits you.'' They climbed a short flight of stairs and crossed to the next wing. ''You said Gabriella would be here soon. Is the whole family coming today?''

''In force, this afternoon.''

Hannah relaxed a little. It would be easy to transfer the package to Reeve and continue on with the plan. ''Has Bennett put his treasure in the vault?''

''Treasure? Oh, his yo-yo.'' With her first easy laugh of the day, Eve entered her bedroom. ''He adores that child, you know. I've never known anyone quite as good with children as Bennett. He puts an enormous amount of time into the Aid for Handicapped Children even though it takes away from his free days with his horses.'' She walked into the adjoining dressing room as she spoke. ''Another reason I suppose I've been moody is that I know Bennett should be on top of the world right now, and he looks as though he rarely closes his eyes.''

''On top of the world?''

"It's taken him six months and a lot of frustration to get approval for the children's wing in the museum. He finally pushed it over the top at the board meeting the other night, but not without a lot of work and fast talking. He didn't mention it to you?"

"No," she said slowly. "No, he didn't mention it."

"It's been his pet project for a couple of years. It took him months to find the right architect, one who'd mesh practicality with the essence of what Bennett wanted to do. Then, because the board wouldn't give an inch, he had the plans drawn up at his own expense. They're wonderful." Eve came back into the room carrying a long box. "You should ask him to see them sometime. He wanted it open, lots of windows so that the kids wouldn't feel closed in. The board mumbled and grumbled when he talked of sculptures the children could make contact with and illustrations from storybooks instead of Rubenses and Renoirs and Rodins under glass."

"I didn't realize he was so... involved."

"Whatever Bennett does he does with total involvement. His idea was to introduce children to art through media they could understand and enjoy. Then there's a section that's reserved for paintings and models the children make themselves."

Eve set the box on the bed and smiled. "I'm surprised he didn't tell you about it. Usually no one's safe. It's taken him two years of planning and six months of fighting to get this project off the ground."

"It sounds lovely." She felt her heart twist and expand and fill with more love. "One often thinks of him as a man only interested in horses and the next party."

"He enjoys the image, but there's more to Bennett than that. I thought that the two of you had gotten quite close."

"Bennett's very kind."

"Hannah, don't disappoint me." A little tired, Eve sat on the edge of the bed. "He watches you walk out of a room and waits for you to come into one."

"He does?"

"Yes." Now she grinned. "He does. With all the anxiety and all the tension of the last weeks, at least I've had the pleasure of seeing Bennett fall in love. You do care, don' you?"

"Yes." It was almost over. Some deceptions were no longer necessary. "I've never known anyone like him."

"There isn't anyone like him."

"Eve, I don't want you to think, or to hope, for some thing that isn't going to happen."

"I'm entitled to think and hope as I choose." She laid hand on the box beside her and patted the lid. "But for now open your present."

"Is this a royal command or a request?"

"Whatever it takes to get you to open it. Please, I'm dy ing to see if you like it."

"Well, it's against my principles to open a present befor Christmas, but..." Giving in, Hannah lifted the lid. Sh pushed aside the layers of tissue paper, then stood staring.

It glittered like a jewel and shimmered like fire. The dres was the rich, luscious green of emeralds with thousands an thousands of tiny beads that caught the afternoon light.

"Take it out," Eve insisted, then too impatient for Han nah, drew it out of the box herself.

The silk swayed, whispered and settled. It was cu straight, with a high neck that glistened with its beaded ban at the throat. The arms would be bare well onto the shoul ders as would the back before the material draped again an followed a long line to the floor. It was a dress made to glit ter under chandeliers and shimmer under moonlight.

"Tell me you like it. I've driven the dressmaker crazy fo a month."

"It's beautiful." Tentatively Hannah reached out. The dress shivered with life at the barest touch. "Eve, it's the most beautiful thing I've ever seen. I don't know what to say."

"Say you'll wear it to the Christmas Ball." Delighted with herself Eve turned Hannah toward the mirror and held the dress in front of her. "Look what it does to your eyes! I knew it." Laughing, she pushed the dress into Hannah's hands so she could step back and take it in. "Yes, I was sure of it. With that skin of yours... Oh yes," she said as she tapped a finger to her lips. "Bennett's going to take one look and babble like an idiot. I can't wait to see it."

"I don't think I should—"

"Of course you should, and you will because I refuse to take no for an answer." She stepped forward, eyes narrowed to pull free a lock of Hannah's hair. "My hairdresser's going to have a whack at you, too."

"That sounds a little ominous." As much as she longed to, she couldn't let herself go. The plain and proper Lady Hannah Rothchild wouldn't have had the nerve to wear such a dress. "Eve, it's lovely, you're lovely, but I don't think I'm made for a dress like this."

"I'm never wrong." Eve brushed off denials with a careless flick of her wrist. She may have only been a princess for two years, but she'd always been determined. "I've spent too long in the theater not to know what suits and what doesn't. Trust me, and if that's too much, do me a favor as a friend."

They *had* become friends, no matter what the initial reasons were or the ultimate goal. What harm would it do to accept? It was very possible that she wouldn't even be in Cordina for the ball. "I'll feel like Cinderella," she murmured, and wished it could be so.

"Good. And you should remember the clock doesn't always strike twelve."

* * *

But it did. Hannah remembered Eve's words as she and
Reeve moved silently through the palace. The game was almost up, and so was her time.

The package had contained the explosives she'd requested and a coded message. She was to make her move
that night and meet Deboque's agent at the docks at one
a.m. The payoff would come then.

"This has to work," Hannah muttered as she carefully set
the first charge. The equipment she used now was ISS-
approved. The package she'd received was already being
traced. Deboque would soon lose Athens and very much
more.

"From outside the walls, it'll look as though the fire's
burning out of control," Reeve said, working as quickly an
competently as she. "The blasts are rigged for more noise
than power. We'll blow out a few windows and put on a hell
of a show while Malori and his men will remain here to bank
it if necessary."

"Is the prince with them now?"

"Yes, Armand is filling the rest of the family in. Malor
objects, but I think you're right. No harm can come from
them knowing what's under way at this point, and a lot of
anxiety can be relieved." He thought of Gabriella. After
tonight, perhaps even the nightmare would fade.

"I couldn't bear to think of Eve waking up to the explosion and thinking it Deboque's doing. And Bennett? He's
safe in the family wing?"

"Bennett's safe," he said, and left it at that. "I'm giving
you ten minutes. That's enough time for you to get off the
grounds. The dock's secure, so that if anything goes down
there, we'll be on top of you. I'll be on the boat that ha
Deboque's yacht under surveillance. We'll move in the moment we have your signal. Hannah, I know the wire's risky.
If you're searched—"

"If I'm searched, I'll deal with it." The mike was an ISS masterpiece that resembled an intricately worked locket that rested inches below the pulse in Hannah's throat.

"If he sees through this, he'll move fast."

"I'll move faster." She laid a hand on his when he started to speak again. "Reeve, I have a stake in this too. I don't want to die."

He looked at her for a moment as a woman. "I have a reputation for keeping my partners alive."

She was grateful he could make her smile. "I'm counting on it. But if something goes wrong, would you give Bennett a message for me?"

"Of course."

"Tell him . . ." She hesitated, unused to trusting her feelings to anyone. The clock struck the hour, midnight, and she prayed the magic would hold. "Tell him I loved him, both parts of me loved him. And there are no regrets."

She left through the main door and drove slowly toward the gates. In minutes, the guards who'd not been informed of the camouflage would react in precisely the way it was expected. Anyone watching the palace would see the shock and the action. For now, she passed through the gates with only the briefest of checks.

She kept an eye on her watch as she drove, hearing the minutes tick off and thinking of Bennett. He would be safe now. Whatever happened that night, he and his family would be safe. If Deboque paid her, he would be arrested for conspiracy. If he killed her, he would be arrested for the murder of an ISS agent. The end justified the means.

Hannah stopped the car, waited and heard the explosion. Malori had promised loud, and had delivered. She opened the door and stood beside the car a moment. The palace was a dim white blur against the night sky, but the east wing was lit like day. The fire was impressive from here, and knowing that none of Deboque's men could get much

closer, she was satisfied. Within twenty minutes one of Malori's men would leak word that the Royal Family, save Armand, had perished in the explosion.

By the time she arrived, the docks were deserted. Word of
trouble had already spread this far. Hannah parked her car
in the shadows, then left it behind to wait in the light. She
made an excellent target.

The boat anchored off the coast appeared to be a small,
expensive pleasure yacht. Several times during the day, a
dark-haired woman had appeared on deck, to sun, to read.
From time to time, she'd been joined by a man, bare
chested, young, bronzed. They'd sipped wine, cuddled,
slept. The watch on the *Invincible* had kept it under surveillance, and had taken bets as to whether the two lovers
would have sex under the sun. They'd been disappointed.

Belowdeck, the ISS had everything from television monitors to grenade launchers. Eight men and three women
crowded into the hulled-out cabin and waited.

Bennett had been confined to the cabin since an hour after dawn. For the past three hours, he'd swallowed nothing
but coffee and impatience. He'd watched the monitor until
his eyes had blurred. Not once had Deboque appeared in the
focus of the long-range camera. He wanted to see him. By
God, he wanted to look into his eyes as the trap snapped
shut. But more, so much more, he wanted to hear over the
transmitter that it was done, and Hannah was safe.

"MacGee's boarding." The man with the headphones
spoke, and continued to smoke. Seconds later, Reeve slipped
into the already crowded cabin. He was dressed in black
from head to foot. Even his face and hands were smeared
with it. He took off his sailor's cap and tossed it aside.

"First stage is finished." He nodded toward Bennett.
"From beyond the gates, it looks as though the east wing is
devastated. The ISS is theatrical."

"The family," Bennett asked as he looked back to the monitor.

"Safe."

He reached for the bitter, cooling coffee beside him. "Hannah?"

"Word should be coming in within minutes. Some of our best men are on the docks as backup."

Bennett shot him a look that held for a long moment. He'd wanted to be at the docks, as close by as possible. He'd run into the stone wall of his father, Reeve and Malori on that, and eventually had had to concede. If he'd been spotted, the entire operation would have been put in jeopardy.

Now it was only Hannah, he thought, only Hannah who risked it all.

"Deboque hasn't been seen all day."

"He's there." Reeve lit a cigarette and prepared to wait. "He wouldn't want to be too far away tonight."

"Contact." An agent on the port side of the cabin lifted a hand to his headphones. "She's made contact."

The breeze off the water was cool and the night was clear. Hannah recognized the man who approached her as the one who had come into the smoky little bar. He came alone and empty handed.

"*Mademoiselle.*"

"My part of the bargain is met, *monsieur*. You have the compensation?"

"It's a nice night for a ride on the water.".

The yacht. She felt a ripple that was both unease and excitement. "You understand I'm no longer in the position to return to Cordina?"

"This is understood." He gestured toward a small motorboat. "Your needs will be seen to."

As before, she had a choice. She could draw her weapon now and take him in. If luck was with them, he would trade his own freedom for Deboque's. She couldn't risk Bennett's safety to luck. Without a word, she stepped into the boat and sat.

Her life was in her own hands now, Hannah thought, and folded them. However the night turned out, Deboque would be ruined.

Her contact didn't speak again, but his gaze shifted back and forth over the dark water. They were all waiting and watching now. Because the night was clear, Deboque's yacht stood out white and stark on the sea. She could see three men on deck, Ricardo and two others. It was Ricardo who assisted her onto the yacht.

"Lady Hannah, it's a pleasure to see you again."

There was something in his eyes, something smirking and self-satisfied. She knew then, as surely as if he'd held a knife to her throat, that she wasn't meant to leave the *Invincible*. Her voice was cool and calm when she spoke, and she hoped, clearly received across the span of water.

"Thank you, Ricardo. I hope this won't take long. I'm forced to admit I'm uneasy in Cordinian waters."

"We sail in an hour."

"For?"

"A more comfortable climate. The radio has announced the tragic deaths of several members of the Royal Family. Prince Armand is grieving in seclusion."

"Of course. Cordina is left without its heart, and without its heir. Monsieur Deboque has been informed?"

"He waits for you in his cabin." Ricardo reached out a hand for Hannah's bag.

"Are employees always searched, Ricardo?"

"We can dispense with that, Lady Hannah, if you will allow me to hold your weapons." He drew out her pistol and pocketed it. "And your knife?"

With a shrug, Hannah lifted her skirt to her thigh. She watched Ricardo's gaze dip and hold there as she drew out the knife. She pushed the release. On either side of her guns clicked.

"An admirable weapon," she said mildly as she held the blade up to the light. "Quiet, stylish, utilitarian." She smiled and sent the blade sliding back into place. "And one I would hardly use on the man who is about to give me five million American dollars." She dropped the knife into Ricardo's palm, knowing she had only her wits as defense now. "Shall we go? I enjoy the smell of money when it's still warm."

He took her arm in his surgeon's hand and with considerable panache, led her belowdeck to Deboque's cabin.

"Lady Hannah." The cabin was lit with a dozen candles. It was a Beethoven sonata this time that poured gently through the speakers. He wore a burgundy jacket and rubies. Blood colors. A magnum of champagne sat nestled in a silver bucket. "How prompt you are. You may leave us, Ricardo."

Hannah heard the door shut behind her. She didn't have to be told Ricardo would be stationed outside it.

"A pleasant ambience," she stated. "Most business isn't transacted in candlelight."

"There's no need for formalities between us now, Hannah." He was smiling as he moved to the champagne. "The announcements from Cordina are a bit hysterical and tragic." The cork rushed out. Wine bubbled to the lip. "I felt a small, tasteful celebration was in order."

"I rarely refuse champagne, *monsieur*, but its taste goes down so much more smoothly when I have money in my hand."

"Patience, my dear." He filled two tulip glasses and offered one. His face was marble pale in the dim light, his eyes almost black and full of pleasure. "To a job well done and a rich, rich future."

She touched her glass to his then sipped. "An excellent vintage."

"I've come to understand you prefer the excellent, and the expensive."

"Precisely. *Monsieur*, I hope you won't be offended if I say while I appreciate the wine and soft light, I would appreciate them more after our business is completed."

"So mercenary." He ran his fingers down her cheek. The candlelight flattered her, he thought. In time she would bloom under his hands. A pity he couldn't take the risk and keep her with him for a few months. He had only an hour for her. But much could be accomplished in an hour. "You'll forgive me, but my mood is very light. I find myself wanting to celebrate your success, our success."

His hand roamed down her throat, within inches of the microphone. She caught it at the wrist and smiled. "You set the mood, *monsieur*, first by taking my weapons. Do you prefer defenseless women?"

"I prefer amenable women." He lifted his hand to her hair, digging his fingers into its richness. Hannah steeled herself for the kiss. She could show resistance, but not revulsion. "You're strong," he murmured and brought his mouth to hers again. "I prefer that as well. When I take you to bed, you'll give me a fight."

"I'll give you more than that. After I've seen the money."

He tightened his fingers, bringing pain quickly enough so that she gasped. Then they relaxed with his laugh. "Very well, *mon amie cupide*. You will see your money, and then you'll give me something in return."

When he turned his back to reveal a hidden safe, Hannah scrubbed her lips with the back of her hand. "I've already given payment for payment."

"The lives of the Royal Family." He spun the dial as Hannah's heart began to drum. "Five million dollars to assassinate the Bissets. Five million dollars to give me a ful plate of revenge and the sweet dessert of power. Do you think it so much?" His eyes glittered as he turned back to her with a large case. "My dear child, you could have asked ten times as much. For over ten years I've plotted, and twice very nearly succeeded in killing a member of the royal family. Now, for the paltry sum of five million dollars, you have disposed of them all for me."

"That's it," Reeve announced as Deboque's voice came over the receiver. "Move in. Slowly."

Bennett's hand closed over his brother-in-law's. "I board with you."

"It's out of the question."

"I board with you," Bennett repeated in a hard, icy voice. Moment by moment, he had listened and sweated as Hannah stood alone with Deboque. As Deboque put his hands on her. As Deboque prepared to pay her for the murder of everything and everyone he loved. "Give me a weapon, Reeve, or I go unarmed."

"My orders are to keep you here."

"If it were Brie?" Bennett's eyes were hot and reckless. "If it were Brie, would you stay behind and let others protect her?"

Reeve looked down at the hand closed over his. It was strong and capable. And young. Then he looked into the eyes that were darker than his wife's but that held the same passions. Rising, he took a .45 automatic from the arsenal.

They would move now, Hannah thought and struggled to keep her voice impassive. "Do you tell me this now so I can regret?" She laughed and walked to the desk. "Five million will do me nicely. I plan to invest and to live quietly in Rio for the next few years."

He kept his eyes on hers as he unlocked the case. The money was there, but would be for his own uses. "You have no desire to continue in my employment?"

"Unfortunately, that would be risky for both of us after the events of tonight."

"Yes." His thoughts exactly. But he opened the lid so that she would at least have the pleasure of seeing the money before he killed her.

"Lovely." Clinging to the role, Hannah stepped forward and lifted a thick stack of crisp hundreds. "Do you know how sensual new money smells?" She fanned the stack.

"Indeed." He slid the top drawer of his desk open. Inside was an elegant pearl-handled revolver. He thought it just to kill her with style. He closed his fingers over it when the first shots were heard from above.

Hannah swung toward the door, hoping he would take excitement for alarm. "What game is this?" she demanded. She slammed the lid on the case, and taking the money headed for the door. Her hand closed over the knob.

"Remain still." Deboque warned. The gun was in his hand now and pointed at her heart. A fine film of sweat pearled over his brow as the sound of running feet pounded over their heads. He held the trigger lightly, but didn't press home. Whatever trouble was on deck, he didn't want to draw it down to him. "The case, Hannah."

"A double cross?" Her eyes narrowed as she calculated how much time she dared stall him. "Yes, you would easily have paid me ten times this if you never intended to pay me at all."

"The case." He started toward her, slowly. Fear was blossoming inside him, not of death, not of defeat, but of prison. He would never survive behind bars again.

Hannah waited until he was two feet away, then with both hands on the handle, swung the heavy case at his gun arm.

* * *

Deboque's men, whether in loyalty or fear, fought madly. Gunfire exploded back and forth from the two boats. A spray of bullets from a machine gun smashed in the wood above Bennett's head and sent splinters raining down his back. He watched a man fall over the rail of the yacht and into the water below.

Already the firing from Deboque's side was coming more sporadically, but time was speeding by. And Hannah was still with Deboque. Alive, Bennett told himself as he aimed and fired. She was alive. He'd know if it was otherwise because his heart would have stopped. But there was an urgency churning in him, more than the wild night and the scent of blood. Moving with it, he worked his way to stern and slipped into the water.

The night was rent with shooting and the shouts of men. He saw a man dive from Deboque's yacht and swim frantically toward a shore that was ten miles off. His hand brushed a body that floated face down. ISS or the enemy, he didn't know. While the fighting raged, he swam silently around the yacht.

Because it was nearly over, Reeve signaled for his men to close in. It was then he noticed that Bennett was no longer beside him.

"The prince." His throat went dry with panic. "Where is Prince Bennett?"

"There." One of the men spotted Bennett just before he disappeared around the stern of Deboque's yacht.

"In the name of God," Reeve breathed. "Move in fast. Prepare to board."

There was no one on the starboard side as Bennett dragged himself on deck. There was the occasional blast and rip of bullets, but the shouting had died. He'd spent an hour during that long, endless day belowdeck studying Hannah's diagram of Deboque's yacht. He went to find her.

* * *

She'd managed to knock the gun across the room, but he was faster and stronger than he appeared. Even as she dove after it, Deboque was on top of her. One hand closed over her throat, shutting off her air. Hannah freed one arm and brought her fist into his windpipe. Then both of them were gasping. She reached forward and her fingers scrabbled over the handle of the gun. She swore in both pain and fury as he dragged her back by the hair. For thirty grim and exhausting seconds, they struggled on the cabin floor. Her blouse tore at the seam. Beneath, bruises were already forming. She bloodied his mouth but was frustrated, unable to land a disabling injury.

Wrapped like lovers they rolled toward the gun again. She reached again, nearly grasping it. Out of the corner of her eye, she saw the fist coming and dodged. The blow was glancing, but strong enough to send her reeling. Then she was looking into the barrel of his gun.

She'd prepared herself to die. Struggling for breath, she braced. If she could do nothing else, she could fulfill her vow to spit in his eyes. "I'm an ISS agent. The Bissets are safe, and you've nowhere to run."

She saw the fury come into his eyes. She smiled at him and waited for the bullet.

When Bennett broke into the room, he saw Deboque crouched over Hannah, pointing a gun at her head. It happened in flashes, so quick that immediately afterward he couldn't be sure who had fired first.

Deboque's head swung around. Their eyes met. As the gun swiveled from Hannah's head toward Bennett's, she screamed and swung out. Two triggers were pressed. Two bullets exploded.

Bennett felt one whiz by him, so close that his skin shuddered and heated from it. He saw the blood bloom on Deboque's chest an instant before he crumpled onto Hannah.

She started shaking then. All the years of training dissolved as she lay trembling under the dead man. She'd prepared for her own death. That was duty. But she'd seen the bullet smash into the wood less than an inch from Bennett's face.

Even when he came to her, pushing what had been Deboque aside and gathering her close, the trembling didn't pass. "It's over, Hannah." He cradled her, rocked her, pressed kisses to her hair. "It's over now." Instead of the satisfaction, even the glory he'd expected to feel there was only relief. She was safe. And he was going to see that she stayed that way.

"You might have been killed. Damn you, Bennett, you were supposed to be home."

"Yes." He glanced up as Reeve rushed into the room. "We'll both go there soon."

There were tears on her cheeks. Brushing them aside, Hannah struggled to stand. She faced Reeve, but had to draw several breaths. "I'm ready to make my report."

"The hell with that." Bennett swept her into his arms. "I'm taking her home."

Epilogue

She'd slept around the clock. It wasn't until over twenty-four hours had passed that Hannah realized that Dr. Franco, the Bissets' personal physician, had given her a sedative.

She'd woken rested and resentful. And though she'd hated to admit it, aching.

The doctor had fussed for another full day, murmuring over her bumps and bruises in his kind but implacable tones. Because his orders to keep her in bed had come from His Royal Highness, neither doctor nor patient had a choice but to obey.

She complained. Even though visitors came often, she fidgeted at the inactivity. Word was delivered through Reeve from ISS headquarters, word that should have delighted her. Deboque's operation had crumbled. She'd been given her promotion. Hannah sulked in bed and wished for escape.

It was Eve who ultimately provided it on the night of the Christmas Ball.

"You're awake. Wonderful."

"Of course I'm awake." Cranky from two days in bed, Hannah shifted. The fact that her ribs were still sore to the touch only made it worse. "I'm going crazy."

"I'm sure you are." Smiling, Eve sat on the edge of the bed. "And I'm not going to embarrass you by going on again about how grateful we all are for everything you did. What I'm going to do is give you Dr. Franco's latest orders."

"Oh, spare me."

"Which are, to get up, get dressed and dance until dawn."

"What?" Hannah pushed herself up, wincing only a little. "I can get up? Do you mean it?"

"Absolutely. Now here." Rising, she lifted Hannah's robe. "Put this on. My hairdresser's expected any minute and she's going to do her magic on you first."

"Magic." With a sigh, Hannah lifted a hand to her hair. "More like a miracle at this point. Eve, as much as I want to get up and be doing, I don't think the ball is the best idea."

"It's the perfect idea." After helping Hannah into her robe, she leaned over to smell the clutch of gardenias by the bedside. "From Bennett?"

"Yes." Hannah gave in enough to touch the waxy leaves with her fingertips. "He brought them this morning. I haven't seen a great deal of him." Shaking off the mood, she stuck her arms through the sleeves. "I know how busy you've all been, with the press conferences and public statements to clear up the entire mess."

Eve lifted a brow. She decided against telling Hannah that Bennett hadn't moved from her bedside throughout the first night. There was enough romance in her for her to want them to discover each other for themselves.

"Speaking of messes, you should see the east wing. Mostly glass. It'll take the maids weeks to get it all. Hannah." On a long breath, Eve took both her shoulders. "I'm going to embarrass you. I know it was an assignment, but whatever reasons brought you to us, you've given us peace. There's nothing I can say or do that can repay that. My child..." She smiled a little. "Marissa and this one are safe. I know what Deboque had planned to do."

"It's over now, Eve."

"Yes." Solemn, Eve kissed both of Hannah's cheeks. "I owe you my life, and the lives of all of my loved ones. If there's anything I can ever do, and I speak as your friend and as the wife of the heir of Cordina, you have only to ask.''

"Put it behind you, and me. Eve, I've never been able to make and keep friends. I'd like to feel that's changed.''

Eve studied the woman she was just beginning to know. "I have two sisters, the one I was born with and the one was given by Alexander." She held out a hand. "I'd like to have three.''

"Your Highness." One of the young maids hovered at the doorway. "I beg your pardon, but Madame Frissoutte is here.''

"Wonderful." Eve hooked her arm through Hannah's. "Prepare to be transformed.''

It was a transformation, Hannah thought as she studied herself in the glass. Her hair, curled wild as a gypsy's down her back, was caught away from her face with two glittering combs. The dress sparkled and shimmered as it draped from her throat to her ankles. She was clever enough with makeup to have covered the bruises on her arms and face.

All she needed were glass slippers, she thought with a half laugh. More illusion. But if this was to be her last night with Bennett, she would take it. There would be no regret when the clock struck twelve.

There was already music in the ballroom. Hannah slipped in, as was her habit, and absorbed the brilliance. Mirrors were polished to reflect the glitter and glamor of gowns and jewels. Chandeliers shone like stars. It was all shimmering silver and icy blue with draping garlands and shiny balls. On a tree that towered to twenty feet were a thousand crystal angels that caught the light.

He'd been watching for her. Waiting. When he saw her the breath simply left his body. The couple he'd been chat-

ing with fell silent, brows lifting as he walked away without a word.

He caught both her hands even as she dipped into a
curtsy. "My God, Hannah." For the first time in his life his
tongue tied itself into knots. "You're exquisite."

"It's Eve's doing." He wore dress whites, with the insignia of his rank and a sword at his side. However many ways
he remembered him, and she knew there would be many,
he would never forget how he looked just now. "Everything is so beautiful."

"It is now." His hand slipped around her waist as he
swirled her into the waltz.

It was magic, she thought. The music, the lights, the mirrors. For hours they danced together, spinning around and
round the room, leaving the food and the wine for others.
When he circled her out to the terrace, she didn't object.
There were still a few minutes until midnight.

Drawing away, she went to the rail to look out at Cor-
ina. Lights glowed in festive colors for the holiday. The
breeze held a springtime warmth and scent.

"Do you ever tire of looking at it?"

"No." He stood beside her. "I think it means even more
now."

She understood, but wanted to keep even Deboque's
ghost at bay. "In England, it would be cold, sleeting. There
might be snow by morning, or we'd have gray, heavy skies.
All the fires would be lit and the rum warmed. The cooks
would have all the puddings and turkeys cooking so that
you'd smell Christmas everywhere."

"We can't give you snow." He lifted her hand and kissed
. "But we could offer the fire and warm rum."

"It doesn't matter." She drew a deep breath. "When I'm
home, I'll remember standing here with Christmas almost
upon us. I'll remember it smelled like roses and jasmine."

"Would you wait here a moment?"

"All right."

"Just here," he said, and kissed her hand again. "I'll on
be a minute."

When he was gone, she turned back to look out again
the lights and the sea. She would be home in a few days, an
in time, perhaps Cordina would seem like a dream. Co
dina, she thought, but never Bennett. She lifted her face
a star but didn't dare wish.

"I have something for you."

With a half smile, she turned, then caught the scent. "O!
chestnuts!" With a laugh, she took the bag he offere
"And they're warm."

"I wanted to give you something from home."

She looked up. There was so much to say, and nothin
that could be said. Instead, she rose on her toes to kiss hin
"Thank you."

He brushed his fingers over her cheek. "I'd thougl
you'd share."

Hannah opened the bag and with her eyes closed, drew i
the scent. "Isn't it wonderful? Now it feels like Chris
mas."

"If Cordina can be enough like home, perhaps you'
stay."

She opened her eyes, then lowered them quickly to tl
bag. "I have orders to return at the end of the week."

"Orders." He started to reach for her, but held himse
back. "Your position in the ISS is important to you." H
couldn't prevent the trace of resentment. "I'm told you r
ceived a promotion."

"A captaincy." She bit her bottom lip. "I'll be workin
behind a desk for a good while. Giving orders." She mar
aged to smile.

"Have you ever considered giving it up?"

"Giving it up?"

It was the blank, puzzled look that worried him. Was it possible she could think of nothing else but her duty to her organization? "If you had something to replace it. Is it the excitement that pulls you?" He cupped her face in his hand, turning it toward the light so that the bruise Deboque had put there showed in a shadow.

"It's simply what I do." She drew a breath. "Bennett, we never talked about what happened on the yacht. I never thanked you for saving my life. I suppose it's because I've been used to taking care of myself."

"I would have killed him for this alone," he murmured as he traced the bruise on her cheek. She started to step back, but a look from him stopped her. "Don't back away from me. I haven't spoken before this because Franco was concerned with keeping you quiet and undisturbed. But dammit, I'll speak of it now."

He stepped closer so she could feel it, the recklessness, the barely controlled fury. "I had to sit and wait and listen to you deal with that man. I had to stay where I was, helpless while you were alone with him. And when I broke into that cabin and saw him holding a gun at your head, I had one hideous flash of what life would be like if you weren't in it. So don't back away from me now, Hannah."

"I won't." She steadied her breathing then laid a calming hand on his. "It's over, Bennett. The best thing for everyone is to put it aside. Cordina is safe. Your family is safe. And so am I."

"I won't accept your risking your life again for anyone."

"Bennett—"

"I won't." He caught her hair in his hands and kissed her, but this time with a force and power that left her breathless. He dragged himself away, reminding himself he had a plan and meant to see it through. "Are you going to try those chestnuts or just stand there smelling them?"

218 *The Playboy Prince*

"What?" She had the bag locked in a viselike grip. She swallowed and opened it again. "I'm sure they're wonderful," she began, knowing she was going to babble. "It was so thoughtful of you to…" She broke off when she reached in and touched a small box. Puzzled, she drew it out.

"There's an American tradition. A box of candied popcorn with a prize in it. I had an urge to give you your Christmas present early."

"I've always been very strict about waiting until Christmas morning."

"I could make it a command, Hannah." He touched her cheek again. "I'd rather not."

"Well, since it *is* the Christmas Ball." She opened the lid and for the first time in her life felt faint.

"It was my grandmother's. I had it reset but it meant more to me to give you this than to choose another from a jeweler." He touched her hair, just the ends of it with his fingertips. "She was British, like you."

It was an emerald, fiery, stunning, made only more brilliant by the symphony of diamonds that circled it. Just looking at it made her light-headed. "Bennett, I couldn't take something like this. It belongs in your family."

"Don't be thick-headed." He took the bag from her to set it on the wall. The scent of chestnuts mixed with the summer fragrance of roses. "You know very well I'm asking you to marry me."

"You—you're carried away," she began, and this time did step back from him. "It's everything that's happened. You're not thinking clearly."

"My mind's never been more clear." He took the box from her, slipped the ring out and tossed the container aside. "We'll do it my way then." Taking her hand, he pushed the ring on. "Now, I can drag you back inside and announce our engagement—or we can talk about it reasonably first."

"Reasonably." How was it she needed to laugh and cry at the same time? "Bennett, you're being anything but reasonable."

"I love you—unreasonably then." He pulled her into his arms and covered her mouth with his. He could feel her heart thud, hear her breath shudder, taste both need and fear. "I'm not letting you go, Hannah, not now, not tomorrow, not ever. You'll have to exchange captain for princess. Believe me, it can be every bit as wearing."

Was it magic, or was it a dream come true? Her head was still spinning as she tried to get a grip on common sense. "You know I'm not the woman you cared for. Please, Bennett, listen to me."

"Do you think I'm a fool?" He spoke so mildly she was deceived into thinking him calm.

"Of course I don't. I only mean that—"

"Shut up." He caught her face in his hands, and she saw by his eyes he was anything but calm. "I thought the woman I first fell in love with was an illusion." He gentled as he brushed his lips over her cheeks. "I was wrong, because she's right here. There was another woman who made my mouth dry every time I looked." His kisses were more urgent now, more possessive. "She's here as well. It's not every man who can love two women and have them both. And I will have you, Hannah."

"You already have me." She was almost ready to believe it could be real, and true and lasting. "But even you can't command a marriage."

He lifted his brow, arrogant, confident. "Don't be too sure. You told me once you wanted me. Was it a lie?"

"No." She steadied herself with two hands on his chest. She was crossing a line in her life, one that allowed for no deceptions. He was offering her a chance to be herself, to love openly and honestly. "No, it wasn't a lie."

"I ask you now if you love me."

She couldn't speak. From deep within the palace the clock began to strike. Midnight. She counted off the gongs and waited for the illusion to fade. Then there was silence and she was still in his arms. Looking down, she saw the ring glow against her finger. A promise. A lifetime.

"I love you, and nothing's ever been more true."

"Share my home." He caught her ring hand in his and pressed his lips to the palm.

"Yes."

"And my family."

She twined her fingers with his. "Yes."

"And my duty."

"From this moment."

She wrapped her arms around him. She lifted her face for his kiss. Below and as far as eyes could see, Cordina spread out before them and prepared to sleep.

* * * * *

Take 4 bestselling love stories FREE

Plus get a FREE surprise gift!

Silhouette

SPECIAL EDITION ™

Nora Roberts

CONVINCING ALEX

Those Wild Ukrainians

Look who Detective Alex Stanislaski has picked up....

When soap opera writer Bess McNee hit the streets in spandex pants and a clinging tube-top in order to research the role of a prostitute, she was looking for trouble—but not too much trouble.

Then she got busted by straight-laced Detective Alex Stanislaski and found a lot more than she'd bargained for. This man wasn't buying anything she said, and Bess realized she was going to have to be a *lot* more convincing....

If you enjoyed TAMING NATASHA (SE #583), LURING A LADY (SE #709) and FALLING FOR RACHEL (SE #810), then be sure to read CONVINCING ALEX, the delightful tale of another one of THOSE WILD UKRAINIANS finding love where it's least expected.

SSENR

SPRING fancy '94

**They're sexy, single...
and about to get snagged!**

Passion is in full bloom as love catches
the fancy of three brash bachelors. You won't
want to miss these stories by three of
Silhouette's hottest authors:

**CAIT LONDON
DIXIE BROWNING
PEPPER ADAMS**

Spring fever is in the air this March—
and there's no avoiding it!

Only from

Silhouette®
™
where passion lives.